PARADISE PRAIRIE

Center Point
Large Print

Also by Allan Vaughan Elston and available from Center Point Large Print:

Forbidden Valley
Grand Mesa
Wyoming Manhunt
Showdown
Gun Law at Laramie
Wagon Wheel Gap

**This Large Print Book carries the
Seal of Approval of N.A.V.H.**

PARADISE PRAIRIE

ALLAN VAUGHAN ELSTON

CENTER POINT LARGE PRINT
THORNDIKE, MAINE

This Center Point Large Print edition
is published in the year 2024 by arrangement with
Golden West Inc.

Copyright © 1969, 1971 by Allan Vaughan Elston.

All rights reserved.

First published in the US by Berkley.

The text of this Large Print edition is unabridged.
In other aspects, this book may vary
from the original edition.
Printed in the United States of America
on permanent paper sourced using
environmentally responsible foresting methods.
Set in 16-point Times New Roman type.

ISBN 979-8-89164-142-6 (hardcover)
ISBN 979-8-89164-146-4 (paperback)

The Library of Congress has cataloged this record
under Library of Congress Control Number: 2024930689

PARADISE PRAIRIE

I

The tree line of East Birch Creek came in sight after Kent Durwin had ridden three hours south out of Pendleton. He spurred to a canter and presently the trees took form. A ranch layout in the shade of a cottonwood grove should be the old Costain place. After riding on up to it Durwin kept his saddle for a minute, critically appraising a square log house with a stone chimney, a sizable barn, sheds, corrals, and a pulley well. No one had lived here, they'd told him at Pendleton, since the Bannock Indian War of 1878; and this was the summer of 1880.

Durwin took from his pocket an advertisement which he'd clipped from the *Rocky Mountain News* at Denver and which had brought him by train and stagecoach a thousand miles here to Umatilla County, in eastern Oregon. He read it again.

> FOR SALE: improved 640-acre ranch 15 miles south of Pendleton, Oregon; on never-failing stream with good ditch right; first class buildings; best stock country in America; price, $12,000.00. See D. Madigan, Pendleton.

It was twice the sum Durwin could raise. He'd supposed the place could be bought with a moderate down payment and terms for the balance. Not till he'd arrived in Pendleton had he learned that a buyer would need to pay all cash. However Kent wasn't sorry he'd come.

He rode to a spruce pole corral and tied his mount there. No doubt the spruce poles had come from the Blue Mountains, whose timbered outline he could see off to the east beyond the Umatilla Indian Reservation. A man could summer his cattle in those high, cool hills and bring them home fat in the fall.

D. Madigan, attorney for the Costain estate, had loaned Kent a key. Before going in he circled the house curiously, aware of the tragic circumstances under which it had last been occupied— the brutal massacre of its three defenders, just two years ago this summer.

A war party of Piutes, Snakes, and Bannocks had surrounded the house, shooting hundreds of rifle bullets into its walls and windows. The three Costains, two men and a teen-age boy, had in the end been shot dead and mutilated. For pure spite, a wrangle pony and two milch cows in a corral had been wantonly slaughtered.

Circling the house Kent was able to see numerous bullet holes in the log walls. Windowpanes, which had been shattered in the attack, were now replaced.

Using his key Kent went inside and found four rooms, the front one with a stone fireplace. The Costain furniture, musty and dusty, was still here. It was a solid, well-built house, the inner walls plastered. The walls were pitted with bullet holes from the raid two years ago.

At Pendleton Kent Durwin had looked up an 1878 newspaper and read an account of that raid. Luther Costain, a widower, had manned an east window and had been found dead on the floor by it. Rick, his bachelor brother, had manned a west window and judging by the empty rifle shells around his body he must have fired many rounds during the last hour of his life. And Bud, Luther's seventeen-year-old son, had used a .32 caliber rabbit rifle to defend a north window.

It made a pattern with other raids in the area. Down on Camas Prairie, south of here, the Winkler ranch had been raided by a party of Piutes. Only John Winkler himself had been killed, because the day before he'd sent his family to Pendleton for safety. Even at Pendleton most of the women and children had been sent down the Columbia River to The Dalles until the raids were over. At Pilot Rock, four miles down Birch Creek from here, all women and children had been evacuated and the men had thrown up a stockade in preparation for an attack which never came. Then, in early fall, organized militia and volunteers had put an end to it with a victory over the Indians at the battle of Willow Springs.

All that was history now. The heir to the Costain property, a niece in Michigan, had instructed Attorney Douglas Madigan to sell this Birch Creek ranch. Yet after two years the place was still unsold. Why? Three possible reasons occurred to Kent. The terms, all cash, would balk most prospective buyers. Also the grim past of this house might make some people a bit squeamish about living here.

After inspecting the house Kent looked over the outbuildings. Then he mounted and forded the creek. It ran in clear riffles and he saw trout darting here and there. Most of the section was on the far side of the stream with an irrigation ditch arching around a hay meadow. There was a small fenced pasture. More and more Kent liked the place. Maybe he could persuade the Pendleton agent to sell it on easy terms.

The raiders, two years ago, had taken only what would appeal to Indians. They'd made off with three Costain rifles, ammunition, a jug of whiskey, a pair of ivory-handled skinning knives, and a pouch of money which the brothers had just acquired from a cattle sale. Kent knew that Indians valued money because it could readily be exchanged for ponies, firearms, blankets, and liquor.

When the sun was noon high Kent rode four

miles downcreek to the village of Pilot Rock. There he found a small frame hotel, a saloon, a general store, a one-room school, a livery barn and smithy. While his horse was being fed Kent sounded the liveryman out about land values along Birch Creek.

"Raw land or improved?" the man asked.

"Improved. Like the Costain place upcreek. What do you figure it's worth?"

"Every cent they're askin' fer it, podner. Richest bottom land in Oregon and an A-one house, even if it is full of Injun bullets."

"Were you here two years ago when the Indians raided it?"

"Yep, but we didn't know about it till the next day. A Mexican sheepherder drove a band of sheep downcrik and as he passed the Costain place he saw some dead stock in a corral. Then he saw the windowpanes was shot out. So he looked in the house and there lay all three of the Costains with rifle shells scattered around 'em. Plain as the nose on your face that those pesky Bannocks had come araidin'. Ain't nobody ever doubted it except Doctor McKay."

Kent looked up curiously. "You mean this Doctor McKay thinks it didn't happen that way?"

"Yep. He was actin' coroner that season and he went out there to look at the bodies. Said he didn't believe Injuns did it."

"Why?"

The liveryman shrugged. "I never did hear him say why. He just said he figgered some no-good white man did it and rigged it to look like an Injun raid."

Kent stepped into his saddle and rode thoughtfully on toward Pendleton.

In late afternoon he reined into the south end of Main Street. Ahead of him seven blocks of saloons and shops came to an end at a new timber bridge over the Umatilla River. Kent's first stop was at the Pioneer Livery Stable, where he left his rented horse. "I'll want him again tomorrow," he told the stableman.

The board walks along Main were raised a foot above the roadway dust. Every building had its hitchrail and every rail had teams or saddle horses. Mule-drawn and ox-drawn wagons rolled by. The walks were filled with shoppers, idlers, off-duty ranch hands—with here and there a tall-hatted reservation Indian squatting with his back to a store wall. Men in sight outnumbered women six to one. Pendleton, largest trading point in eastern Oregon, now had fifteen hundred people, four general stores, three hotels, two newspapers, three livery stables, a Wells-Fargo office—not to mention fourteen drinking and gambling places. Oddly the town as yet had no bank. Banking was done through a Portland bank, Wells-Fargo transporting checks, currency, and gold back and forth by stagecoach and river boat.

Kent moved on toward the new Villard House, where he'd registered upon his arrival day before yesterday.

When he crossed Alta Street, the entire next block, on the east side of Main, was a public square with a two-story frame courthouse centering it. Opposite the square, on the west side of Main, was the brick Hollister Block, on whose ground floor were the Delmonico Restaurant, the Palace Saloon, and the Blue Front Store; and whose upper floor provided offices for the town's more successful professional men.

Kent Durwin took stairs which led him to this upper floor. On the left of a wide corridor were offices occupied by lawyers and on the right offices occupied by doctors. Douglas Madigan had the front office on the left. Its door was unlocked but when Kent went in he found the office empty. He wanted to sound Madigan out about extending easy terms for the purchase of the Costain property.

After a short wait Kent left the office and as he was about to go down the stairs he noticed lettering on a door to the right.

W. C. McKay, M.D.
E. P. Egan, M.D.
J. W. Hall, M.D.

The door was partly open and through it Kent glimpsed a dark-haired girl in a nurse's uniform sitting at a desk. Perhaps she served as receptionist for all three of the doctors who shared this suite. Looking rearward down the corridor Kent saw four other doors on the right side. The first three had shingles announcing in turn that they were the private offices of McKay, Egan, and Hall. The rearmost door's shingle said: EMERGENCY CLINIC.

Kent remembered what the Pilot Rock liverymen had told him; that a Doctor McKay of Pendleton was the only man in the county who didn't believe Indians had raided the Costain ranch two years ago. He was curious to know why. On an impulse he went into the reception office and spoke to the girl there. "Is Doctor McKay busy?"

"He's out on a call," she said. "Would you like to see Doctor Egan? Or Doctor Hall?"

She was younger than he'd thought, not over twenty, with smiling brown eyes and curls of black hair showing from under her cap. Kent shook his head, grinning a bit sheepishly. "I'm not sick, or anything. Just wanted to ask him a question or two."

"Perhaps I can answer them," the girl offered.

Her smile made Kent want to know her better. He stood there with his hat in his hand, half embarrassed for coming in on a nonmedical errand, half glad because he'd been lonely for the sight of a girl like this one. "I don't reckon you'd know anything about it, Miss."

"Try me and see. You're new in town, aren't you? Won't you sit down?"

He sat down and laid his range hat on his knees. "Rode out to the Costain place on Birch Creek today; had an idea I might take it over and start running stock."

The girl nodded in matter-of-fact approval. "I've heard Doctor McKay speak of the Costain ranch. You wanted his opinion of it?"

"Not exactly. Just wanted to know why he thinks it wasn't Indians who raided the place two years ago."

Her response was prompt. "That's easy. I've often heard him say. Everyone else thinks he's prejudiced, because he's part Indian himself, you know."

"Is he?" Kent echoed in surprise. "I've never met him."

"He's the grandest man I ever knew," she said warmly. "Kind, generous, with a brilliant, liberal mind. His father was Scotch, his mother half Canadian and half Chippewa. Our local Indians trust him and for years he's been the official government surgeon out at the Umatilla agency. It wasn't local Indians who went on the warpath two years ago. The reservation tribes—Cayuse, Umatillas, and Walla Wallas—

are friendly. It was Idaho Indians—Snakes, Piutes, and Bannocks—who came raiding into Oregon."

"But your boss," Kent prompted, "thinks it was white men who killed the Costains?"

"Yes. They shot two milch cows and a corral pony. Doctor McKay thinks that raiding Bannocks would have taken the pony with them, and burned the hay barn."

"What they did take away with them," Kent remembered, "was three rifles, ammunition, two skinning knives, a jug of whiskey and nine thousand dollars the Costains had just got from a beef sale."

"When the war came to an end a few weeks later," the girl said, "more than a hundred Indian prisoners were taken. They admitted many other raids but denied raiding the Costains. A great deal of loot was recovered but it didn't include the Costain rifles or skinning knives."

"Thanks. No use botherin' the doctor now. Maybe he's right. After two years it's not likely we'll ever find out for sure."

"I'll tell him you called, Mr. . . . ."

"I'm Kent Durwin from Colorado, stopping at the Villard House."

"And I'm Nancy Rollins." When Kent stood up she smiled and held out her hand. "I *do* hope you find a place that suits you, Mr. Durwin."

• • •

An hour later Kent had taken a sponge bath in his Villard House room. Freshly shaved, he went down to the lobby. A dining room was on one side and a barroom on the other. After a day in the saddle Kent felt like treating himself to a beer.

The friendly bartender had served him one the evening before and so knew the purpose of Kent's trip to Oregon. "Been out lookin' at land?" he asked.

Kent nodded. "Looked at a Birch Creek property today. Tomorrow I'll take a ride up McKay Creek. I hear there's a half section for sale up that way."

"You'll be makin' no mistake, young fella, if you pick this Umatilla range to run cows on. You see that man back there—the one havin' a drink with Lot Livermore?" The barman thumbed toward two customers at a rear table.

Having called for mail here at Pendleton, Kent knew Postmaster Lot Livermore by sight. The man with him had the look of a successful stockman.

"That's Jerry DeSpain," the barman confided. "He walked into Oregon penniless in 1851; took a job tendin' stock and in a coupla years was runnin' a few head of his own. Right now his brand is on a thousand horses, five thousand cows, and his herders are tendin' ten thousand

17

sheep in the Blue Mountains. Biggest taxpayer in the county, Jerry is. He just finished puttin' up the brick-front DeSpain Block on Alta Street. Made every dime of it outa livestock."

Kent crossed the dining room. After a waitress took his order he looked curiously at the other diners. Two of them caught his eye and held it.

They made a handsome couple. The man was Douglas Madigan, agent for the Costain estate. He was ruddy-faced, powerfully built with a thatch of black hair, clean-shaven except for deep sideburns. Everything about him spoke of professional success.

His dinner guest, Kent saw with a twinge of envy, was the medical receptionist, Nancy Rollins.

II

Kent got an early start and before the sun was an hour high was riding up McKay Creek. Like Birch, McKay Creek was also a tributary of the Umatilla River coming in from the south. Land along it and stretching eastward to the Blue Mountains was part of the Umatilla Indian Reservation—except for a tract here and there which some white settler had purchased in fee simple from a tribesman. The Indians themselves had mainly settled nearer the mountains, or around the Agency a few miles up the Umatilla River from Pendleton.

In the first eight miles of his ride Kent passed three farms, two occupied by white families and one by an Indian.

The half section advertised in a recent Pendleton paper lay twelve miles up McKay Creek. Kent came to it in midmorning and knew at once it wasn't what he was looking for. The improvements were shabby—a sod-roofed shack with a tumble-down shed. As a base on which to build a stock ranch, the Costain section had this place beat ten to one.

Disappointed, Kent sat in his saddle and rolled a cigarette. Someday he hoped to marry and start a family. No particular girl in mind yet, but he was sure there would be in time. A man couldn't live by himself forever. When he found the right girl he wanted to take her to a place he could be proud of. He thought of the ranch he'd looked at yesterday—its cool shade and riffling stream and solid log house with a stone hearth: a right nice place to raise a family.

It would be only an hour's ride southwesterly to the Costain place. Why not take a look at it again? If the lawyer wouldn't agree to terms, he might appeal by letter to the owner herself. A niece in Michigan, they said. After waiting two years to cash in on her inheritance she might be only too glad to accept a down payment and take Kent's note for the balance.

Kent flipped his smoke away and rode southwest, toward East Birch Creek. In all his life Kent had never seen a prettier range than this one. Some of the early settlers had called it Paradise Prairie and Kent, riding across it, could not quarrel with the name.

The sun lacked an hour of noon when he dismounted at the spruce-pole corral of the long-deserted ranch. Again he explored the four-room log house and the hay barn. Again he saw trout darting in the clear waters of the stream. He scooped up a handful of soil and saw that it was rich, sandy loam. Anything would grow here, especially a family.

A man could come home to a place like this,

after a day in the saddle, and be welcomed by supper smoke drifting from that stone chimney. He wouldn't need to worry about Indians raiding again, as they had two years ago.

But had they? There were many who said yes; but there was one who said no. A doctor named McKay, himself one-fourth Indian—a man trusted by all three of the reservation tribes. According to McKay, the raid here had been the work of a white man who'd contrived to make it look like an Indian massacre.

In the warm midday sun Kent sat on the coping of the pulley well and gave it thought. How could a white killer manage a thing like that?

Suppose he'd desperately needed money and knew that the Costains had just made a cash cattle sale. As a friend or neighbor he might call here and ask for a loan; and be turned down. They'd offer him a cup of coffee, perhaps. Maybe it was evening and he'd found the three—a boy with his father and uncle—eating supper. Their rifles would be leaning against a wall, ready for use, since they knew of hostile raids not far south of here.

On guard against Indians, they'd be definitely off guard against a guest sharing a pot of coffee with them. Easy for the guest to pick up one of those repeating rifles and fire three quick shots.

It wouldn't be too hard, then, to make it look like an Indian raid. He'd need to drag each body to a window, as though the man or boy had been defending that window when shot. He'd need to shoot out the windowpanes, scattering empty shells of the right caliber on the floor beside each dead man.

Also he'd need to circle the house and fire many bullets into each outer wall. He'd have to pick up the ejected shells and carry them back to positions on all four sides from which besieging raiders would logically have been firing.

According to newspaper accounts, all the Costain stock had been out on the range except two milch cows and a wrangle pony. The man could shoot them to leave further evidence of wanton savagery, then go in to slash his human victims.

He'd help himself to the cattle money, knowing that raiding Bannocks would have done the same. But raiding Indians would also take certain articles other than money. First of all the three Costain rifles—a Winchester 44-40 center-fire belonging to the father, a .44 rimfire belonging to the uncle, and a .32 rabbit gun belonging to the boy. They'd take all the ammunition for those rifles; also a jug of whiskey.

What else? Furniture, clothing, or cooking utensils wouldn't interest them; but a pair of ivory-handled skinning knives would.

Unless those items were missing from the

house, a sheriff might doubt that there'd been a raid by Indians.

Yet a white killer, Kent reasoned, would be afraid to take the three rifles away with him. They were conspicuous and bulky. If found on him, they'd at once convict him of the crime. He must remove them from the house and then quickly get rid of them.

How could he get rid of them? Kent Durwin pondered it through three cigarettes. The quickest way to get rid of three rifles and a whiskey jug, he concluded, would be to bury them.

Not too near the house, of course. Yet the man would be in a sweat to get away from here and wouldn't dare delay too long. He'd carry the articles at least a hundred yards up or down the creek.

It seemed a forlorn hope that anyone could find a two-year-old burial spot. Grass and weeds, plus two seasons of falling leaves, would have covered the place. Yet a look wouldn't hurt. In any case Kent was here to explore the property; so he took a walk up the creek bank—two hundred yards or more.

Twice he got down on all fours to peer into a hollow log into which a man might have stuffed rifles and a jug. But he hadn't.

Finding nothing upcreek, Kent returned to the house and walked downcreek. The first hundred yards revealed nothing. Beyond that a thicket of wild plum barred the way. A man carrying a spade, three rifles, and a gallon jug would hardly force his way through that thicket. He'd bypass it. So Kent bypassed it; and just beyond, in cottonwood shade not ten yards from the creek bank, he saw in the weeds what looked like a small, tarnished brass cylinder.

He picked it up and saw that it was an unused cartridge for a 44-40 rifle.

A hunter wouldn't throw away this cartridge. It must have been dropped by mistake. What about a killer who'd just destroyed the entire Costain family? A man hurrying afoot down the creek bank encumbered with a spade, three rifles, a heavy jug, two long knives, and all the ammunition he'd found in the house! With his hands more than full, had he dropped one of the cartridges here?

Suppose he'd stopped here, setting aside everything but his spade in order to dig a trench. Once the trench was dug he'd throw everything into it and might easily overlook one cartridge.

Kent dropped on all fours and carefully inspected the ground. A certain rectangle of it, about four feet by two, seemed yellower than the rest. Normally the top soil was black loam but here was a small strip of clay. Undersoil, two or more feet deep, might be clay. In the refilling of the trench, some of the clay might be left on top.

Kent went back to the Costain barn to find

something to dig with. A few odds and ends had been left here: a pitchfork with a broken handle, a branding iron, a rusty irrigation shovel with a split blade.

For Kent's purpose the shovel would do. He took it down the creek and in a few minutes was digging with it at a spot where clay undersoil was showing.

When his excavation was two feet deep his shovel blade struck a metal obstacle. Presently he exposed it—the rust-caked barrel of a rifle.

In another half hour of digging he had the entire evidence exposed. The three missing Costain rifles; a gallon jug still full of whiskey; two ivory-handled skinning knives; one full box of .44 rimfire cartridges; one partial box of 44-40 centerfires; and a handful of .32's.

The shell he'd found above ground had no doubt been spilled from the open box of 44-40's.

Also in the trench Kent found one puzzling item—a thing which shouldn't be here at all. A key with a brass tag on it. The key had an etched number, and when Kent buffed away the dirt and tarnish the number proved to be *60*. The key wasn't the right shape to be a door key. It was flat—more like a padlock or drawer key.

Kent put it in his pocket so that he could show it to the Pendleton sheriff. Most likely the killer had inadvertently dropped it while digging this trench. Sweating from exertion he might take out a handkerchief to mop his face—unintentionally pulling out a key which could fall unnoticed into the hole.

A certain thing was that Doctor McKay had been right. Indians would have made off with these rifles. Only a white man fearful of being incriminated would have gotten rid of them in this way.

The sheriff should see the evidence as Kent himself had found it. So he put the rifles and the jug, the knives and the cartridges back into the trench and refilled it.

By then it was nightfall. He was fifteen miles from Pendleton and it would be close to midnight before he could get there. Back at the corral, Kent tightened his saddle cinch, watered his mount, and rode north toward town.

It was a few minutes short of midnight when he turned his rented horse in at the livery stable. On a bare possibility that the sheriff might be working late at his office, Kent hurried up Main to the courthouse. But the county offices were closed and locked. Should he go to the sheriff's house? Kent decided not to. A secret buried for two years could wait a few hours longer.

He went out to the street and was turning toward the Villard House when he saw a lighted upper window across Main. It was in the brick Hollister Block and he knew that the front office on that side was Attorney Madigan's. Evidently the man was still at his desk, maybe preparing for litigation coming up tomorrow.

Why not go over there and sound him out about selling the Costain ranch on terms? Six thousand dollars down, and a note for six thousand at fair interest. Madigan could do no worse than say no.

Crossing the street Kent went up the Hollister Block stairs to the second-floor hall. All doors there were closed. A darkened office on the right was the medical reception room where Kent had met Nancy Rollins. A lighted office on the left was Madigan's.

On a whimsical impulse Kent took a scrap of paper from his pocket and wrote a line on it.

> Miss Rollins: Your doctor was right and everyone else wrong. K.D.

He slipped it under the reception-room door. Then he knocked on the opposite door and heard Madigan call out, "Come in."

The man was in his shirt sleeves with a half-written brief in front of him. He seemed annoyed at the intrusion. "I'm pretty busy . . ."

"I won't keep you but a minute," Kent said. "Been out twice to look at the Costain place and it suits me fine. If you'll take a reasonable down payment . . ."

"The terms," Madigan broke in brusquely, "are all cash."

For the first time Kent decided he didn't like the man. He wished now he hadn't come up. But since he was here he might as well tell what everyone in town would know by noon tomorrow.

"While I was there I dug up something. Turns out Doctor McKay was right about what happened two years ago."

At once Madigan's manner changed. A shrewd interest showed on his face. "Dug up something? Sit down and tell me about it."

Kent told it in a dozen clipped sentences. "I stopped at the courthouse," he added, "to tell the sheriff. Wanted to show him this." Kent took the brass-tagged key from his pocket and held it in the palm of his hand. "But nobody was over there so I'll tell him in the morning."

Madigan stood up, put on his hat and coat. "A thing like that can't wait till morning," he said crisply. "We'd better go to the sheriff's house and wake him up."

"Okay. Lead the way." Kent went out with Madigan and down to the Main Street walk.

There Madigan turned north. Except for an occasional saloon light the street was dark. They crossed Court Street and beyond that this west side of Main had no lights. Across the east side the Villard House lobby was lighted. And so was the St. Louis Restaurant halfway between Court and Water Streets.

"Sheriff Martin," Madigan said, "lives just the other side of the bridge."

Kent nodded. Having been in Pendleton three days he knew that the entire town was on the south side of the Umatilla River except for a few new residences on higher ground beyond the Main Street bridge.

After passing Lot Livermore's post office, it was only a few steps to the bridge. It was a wooden truss bridge with plank flooring, spanning one of the largest tributaries of the Columbia River. Right now the Umatilla was close to flood tide, eighty yards wide and roaring turbulently under the bridge.

As they neared midbridge Douglas Madigan's hand moved to the left breast pocket of his coat. The .38 revolver he habitually carried there was for defense against footpads when he had to go home late from his office.

At midbridge he dropped a step behind Kent Durwin. Then he struck hard at the back of Kent's head. Kent buckled on the planks near the downstream truss. It took Madigan only a few seconds to retrieve a brass-tagged key from Kent's pocket. This he threw as far as he could into the rapids of the river. He picked up his stunned victim and heaved him over the rail. The torrent beneath was so turbulent that he barely heard the splash. The racing current was sure to carry the body far down the river.

In the midnight dark Madigan hurried back to Main Street. As he passed the post office he remembered with a shiver the address printed at the top of his professional stationery:

DOUGLAS MADIGAN
Attorney-at-Law
Post Office Box 60
Pendleton, Umatilla County, Oregon

III

At eight in the morning Nancy Rollins turned up the stairs leading to the medical suite. A gray, ankle-length coat covered her nurse's uniform. In the upper hall she unlocked the reception-room door and went in. She hung up her coat and from a closet shelf took a crisp, white nurse's cap, standing at a mirror to fit it on her head.

Nancy raised a blind to brighten the office and it was only then that she noticed a scrap of paper near the door. She picked it up and read curiously:

> Miss Rollins: Your doctor was right and everyone else wrong. K.D.

For a moment the *K.D.* meant nothing. Then she remembered the nice-looking young man who'd stopped in to see Doctor McKay late day before yesterday. He'd given the name Kent Durwin. They'd discussed a two-year-old tragedy and she'd told him that only Doctor McKay had disagreed with the popular verdict.

Now here was a note saying the doctor was right. Sometime during the night it had been slipped under this door.

Nancy puzzled over it, then laid it aside. Offices

in this suite had connecting doors and with her feathered brush the girl went from room to room, straightening up and dusting the furniture. First Doctor McKay's office, then Doctor Egan's, then Doctor Hall's. From Hall's office she went through another connecting door into a longer room equipped with two beds, a leather operating table, and other bare necessities of an emergency hospital.

Right now the room was empty, Nancy checked the beds and a cabinet of chemicals, opened a rear window to let in fresh air, then went back to the reception room by way of the public corridor. At this early hour law offices on the left side of the hallway were unoccupied.

At her own desk Nancy reread the K.D. note. Then she heard brisk steps coming up from the street. She knew it was Doctor McKay when she heard him go into the office adjoining her own. After allowing him time to get settled she took the K.D. note and went in to see him. "It was slipped under my door during the night, Doctor."

He was a short, stocky man in his middle fifties, with eyes which beamed with kindliness and intelligence. He wore gold-rimmed glasses, a knee-length coat, a white, starched shirt, and a high, stiff collar. He had the dark eyes and skin and hair of an Indian.

"Who," he asked after reading the note, "is K.D.?"

She told him about Kent Durwin's call late day before yesterday and repeated her conversation with him.

McKay smiled gravely. "So he thinks I'm right. I'd like to see him, Nancy."

"He's only been in town a few days," she said, "and I think he has a room at the Villard House."

"Please go over there, Nancy, and ask him if he has time to see me. I'd go myself, only I'm expecting a patient."

Nancy went down to the front walk. It was only half a block north to the Villard House.

At the registry desk she asked if Kent Durwin was in.

"Haven't seen him come down to breakfast," the clerk said. His bell summoned a boy. "Run up to 206, Eddie, and see if Mr. Durwin's in his room."

In five minutes the boy came back. "I knocked and he didn't answer," he reported. "Door was locked; so I called a chambermaid and she opened it. Nobody there. The bed hasn't been slept in."

"When he comes in," Nancy asked, "will you tell him Doctor McKay would like to see him?"

As she was turning away another boy came in from the street. "Mr. Durwin around?" the boy asked. The name made Nancy stand by to hear more.

"Didn't come in last night," the clerk said. "Any message?"

"I'm from the Pioneer livery barn," the boy said. "They wanta know if Mr. Durwin'll need his saddle horse again today. He used it the last two days."

Nancy put in a question. "What time did he turn the horse in last night?"

"About midnight," the boy said.

So it was midnight or after, Nancy concluded as she went back to the medical offices, when Kent Durwin had slipped the note under her door.

Two patients were in the reception room. It was an hour before Nancy had a chance to report on her errand to the Villard House.

"For some reason Mr. Durwin didn't go to his room last night, Doctor. He left his horse at the livery barn about midnight, then came by here to slip a note under my door. After that . . ." The girl spread her hands in mystification.

For Nancy Rollins home was a cottage on Garden Street which she shared with Amy Brundage, the schoolteacher. She went there for a late lunch, finding that Amy had come and gone. Nancy herself was in a hurry to get back. A disturbing premonition warned her that something unplanned and unpleasant must have happened to Kent Durwin.

Else why, arriving after midnight within a

block of his hotel, would he fail to go there and to bed?

Soon after she got back to her office Nancy heard a commotion from the street. She looked out across Main at the courthouse. Sheriff Martin came running out, followed by Deputies Sargent and Sperry. The sheriff commandeered a spring wagon, got in and whipped the team to a run south down Main. His deputies swung aboard saddle horses and followed.

Curious and excited voices made Nancy open her window to hear better. An off-duty stage driver named Billy Glover yelled a question to Town Marshal Ben Gray. "How far down the river is he, Ben?"

"About half a mile, Billy. Washed ashore there, looks like. Don't know whether they can save him or not. I better go tell Doc McKay to get ready."

A minute later Nancy was showing Gray into McKay's office. "Man in the river, Doc," Gray reported. "As near dead as a guy can get and still be breathin'. He's unconscious, all bruised and bunged up. Sheriff's fetchin' him here in a spring wagon."

"Know who he is, Ben?"

"Card in his wallet says his name's Durwin. Stranger in town. Coupla Cayuse Indians found him half in and half out of the water."

McKay turned briskly to his nurse. "Get things

ready for him, Nancy. Then bring a stretcher down to the street walk."

Shortly a spring wagon drew up in front of the Hollister Block. The county sheriff was driving. Two deputies took a stretcher from the hands of Nancy Rollins. Under the supervision of Doctor McKay what looked like a bedraggled dead man was taken from the wagon and placed gently on the stretcher. The man was fully dressed—coat, boots, and all—the soggy garments clinging to his skin. "Looks like he's been in the water all night," Sheriff Martin reported. "Oughta be long dead; but the current beached him with his head outa water."

Nancy preceded them up the stairs and when they got to the hospital room she had everything ready. One bed was turned back; over the other bed was a canvas, laid so that the patient could be put there while they removed his soggy clothing.

A crowd, including a reporter from the *East Oregonian*, had followed from the street. "Keep them out of here," McKay directed.

Nancy managed to eject everyone except county officers. By then Kent Durwin had been placed on the canvas-covered bed, where they were slipping off his boots and river-soaked clothing.

"His wallet's got money in it," a deputy said,

"Golly whiz! Look at that bump on the back of his head!"

"Somebody must've whanged him," Deputy Bob Sargent added.

"He's bruised from head to foot," McKay reported after a quick examination, "like he'd hit a hundred sharp rocks in the rapids of the river."

"May have a brain concussion," Doctor Egan added. "Not likely he'll be able to tell us anything for a day or two."

"We'll try to get a swallow of brandy down him," McKay decided. "Then we'll wrap him in a warm blanket and put him to bed. Nancy, warm a blanket."

From a linen closet Nancy took a heavy woolen blanket. The nearest hot stove would be in the kitchen of the Delmonico Restaurant on the ground floor of this building. She went down the rear stairs which led to an alley exit. A few steps along the alley took her to the Delmonico's kitchen entrance.

A Chinese cook wasn't surprised when she came in with a blanket. "Somebody have chill, yes?" The cook nodded toward the stove. Nancy unfolded the blanket and held it close to the stove. After a few minutes she reversed her grip to expose the other side of it to the heat. "Somebody get drunk, fall in river?" the cook guessed.

When her blanket was warm on both sides Nancy hurried upstairs with it. By then Kent

Durwin, wearing a flannel hospital gown, lay between linen sheets. McKay turned the cover back and helped Nancy wrap him in the warm blanket. The patient's open eyes had a glazed stare.

"We gotta find out what happened," Sheriff Martin said impatiently. "When can I ask him some questions?"

"Not now," McKay decreed emphatically. "He needs complete rest and quiet."

Deputy Sperry picked up Kent Durwin's soggy clothing and made a bundle of them. "Soon as I get 'em dried out," he promised, "I'll bring 'em back."

Martin turned to the other deputy, Sargent. "Check up and down the street, Bob, and see if you can find out what this boy was doing last night."

Doctor McKay said with calm assurance, "I can tell you what he was doing about midnight."

"Yeh? What?"

"He was slipping this note under my reception-room door." He handed Martin a scrap of paper.

Martin gaped at the signature, *K.D.*

IV

Nancy spent the next hour pacifying patients who had appointments with Doctor McKay. "He's on an emergency," she told them. "Can't you come in tomorrow?"

In midafternoon she went back to the hospital room and found that McKay had completed his examination. Other than a brain concussion there were no serious injuries. "In time he'll recover, I think, both mentally and physically. I want someone to be with him day and night. What about Mrs. Olsen?"

Mrs. Olsen was a widow who sometimes earned a few dollars by sitting up with sick people. She had no medical training but she'd once worked in a San Francisco hospital and knew how to feed a patient or take his temperature.

"When would you want her?" Nancy asked.

"Tonight; and every night till Durwin is ready to be moved to his hotel room. Let's make it a ten-hour shift, nine till seven. Better go right now and see if she's available."

Nancy went out and was back in half an hour. "Mrs. Olsen will be glad to come, Doctor."

"I want you to stay here till six, Nancy. Then Deputy Sargent will relieve you and watch the patient till Mrs. Olsen gets here at nine. Don't bother him with questions; but if he talks of his own accord, take down everything he says. Any minute he might get his wits back and tell what happened."

Nancy settled herself at Durwin's bedside. His eyes were closed now. She couldn't tell whether he was unconscious or asleep.

He'd been in town only three days, hardly long enough to make a deadly enemy. Yet someone had hit him on the head and thrown him in the river. It must have happened after he'd slipped the note under her door—a message dealing with the Costain massacre two years ago.

Nancy kept watch till Deputy Bob Sargent came in. "I'll take over till Mrs. Olsen comes, Nancy. This boy said anything yet?"

"Not a word, Bob. If he says anything be sure to take it down."

Nancy hurried home to her cottage and found Amy Brundage preparing supper. "We've no idea what happened," Nancy told her.

Just before bedtime she put on a cape and went to the Hollister Block. The upper hall was lighted dimly by a wall-bracketed oil lamp. She went back to the ward and found Mrs. Olsen faithfully on watch.

The woman had fitted a shade over the ward lamp. It gave her just enough light to see the patient's face. He'd lain perfectly quiet, she told Nancy. "Doctor McKay brought me a pan of milk. I'm to heat it and feed it, if he comes to hungry. There's no fever."

"I'll be in at seven. Good night, Mrs. Olsen."

At a minute before seven in the morning Nancy arrived at the Hollister Block. As she was about to go up the stairs she almost collided with Douglas Madigan, who came out of the Delmonico Restaurant.

This morning, to her surprise, he wore corduroys and boots, as well as a battered old hat with artificial flies hooked in the band. A saddled horse at the rack had waders and the joints of a bamboo fly-rod tied back of the cantle.

"I've been working too hard, Nancy. Thought I'd take a day off and go fishing."

It wasn't like him, she thought. Doug Madigan wasn't a sportsman. Other Pendleton men often went fishing up McKay or Birch Creek; or went hunting for birds on the prairie. But not Douglas Madigan.

Upstairs she put on the nurse's cap. She was an hour earlier than usual and no patients could be coming in for a while. Right now she must go back and relieve Mrs. Olsen.

"He had a quiet night," the woman told her. "Still no fever. I tried to feed him some milk but he wouldn't take it."

"Go home and get some rest yourself, Mrs. Olsen. And come back at nine tonight."

Nancy raised a blind to let in summer sunlight. Then she heated water and bathed Kent Durwin's face. His eyes were open vacantly. "You're getting better," she said gently. "And you've got the best doctor in Oregon."

Footsteps were coming down the corridor and she recognized them as Doctor McKay's. "Just saw Mrs. Olsen and got her report," he said as he came in. "The sheriff'll be here in a few minutes. I've given him permission to ask three questions. Three and no more."

Sheriff William Martin presently came in and stood looking down at Kent Durwin.

"*Who* hit you?" was his first question.

It brought no response. Durwin's stare was as blank as a child's.

"*Why* did he hit you?" was the next question. Again there was no reaction of any kind.

Martin fired his third and last question. "*Where* did it happen?"

This time a single faint word came from Durwin's lips. A one-syllable word beginning with a *B*.

"You heard it?" the sheriff demanded sharply of McKay. "Sounded like *bridge,* didn't it?"

Nancy's nod was as emphatic as McKay's. Martin was equally sure of it as he smacked fist into palm. "Betcha he was tossed off the Main Street bridge. With the river up and fast like it is, he'd be carried a half mile down the rapids and beached at the first big bend. If he says anything more, let me know."

But Kent didn't say anything more. And while McKay and Nancy watched over him, Martin crossed to the courthouse and prepared for a test.

"Take two grain sacks," he directed Deputy John Sperry. "Stuff 'em full of rags and put in just enough chunks of iron to make 'em weigh two hundred pounds when they're tied together end-to-end. Then fetch 'em to the Main Street bridge."

A crowd of onlookers was assembled on the bridge when Sperry arrived there with the dummy. "It's about the size and weight of a man's body," Martin explained. "Sperry, go down the south bank to the bend half a mile below here where we found Durwin. Set your watch by mine. At exactly nine o'clock, I'll drop this dummy over the rail. Bob, you run along the bank and keep pace with it. Watch where it washes ashore."

At nine-thirty Sheriff Martin was back in McKay's hospital ward. "Durwin was thrown off the bridge, all right. It took a dummy of his weight just six minutes to run those rapids half a mile to the bend. Long enough to batter a man up but not quite long enough to drown him."

The day passed without any further word from Durwin. Deputies from the sheriff's office took turns sitting by the bed. Bob Sargent had dried

Durwin's clothes and brought them back, draping them on hangers by the wall with the boots underneath. Hopefully they'd be ready for him when he was able to be moved to his Villard House room.

The only success of the afternoon came when the patient permitted Nancy to feed him a cupful of broth with a spoon.

At nine o'clock, just after nightfall, Mrs. Olsen relieved Deputy Sargent. Again she lighted a shaded oil lamp which allowed her to see dimly the patient's face. For two hours she sat by the bed, watching, glad that distance dulled the saloon sounds which came from Main Street.

Near midnight she went to the stove and heated a cup of coffee for herself. A rear window gave onto an alley but she could see nothing out there. It was a cloudy, starless night.

Then sounds from the front told her that someone was coming upstairs from the street. More than one person, she concluded. The footsteps approached slowly down the hall; then her door opened and two men were limned in the dimness there. One man was apparently helpless and was being supported by the other. They were shaggy, roughly dressed men with the smell of a barroom on them.

"He's been shot," the erect man announced to Mrs. Olsen. "Ruckus at the Webfoot bar. While

I put him to bed you better go fer a doctor."

She saw a redness at the sagging man's middle and could hardly doubt it was blood. "Very well. But please don't disturb this other patient. I'll have Doctor McKay here soon as I can."

Before she was halfway down the street stairs the taller man was snapping orders. "Gather up his clothes, Murph, boots and all. I see a stretcher over there. We can tote him down on it."

The shorter man, no longer needing support, quickly gathered up the only male garments in sight. They were the boots and dry clothing which had been returned today by Deputy Sargent. In less than a minute Kent Durwin, wrapped in his blankets, was placed on the stretcher. The two men carried him out down the rear stairs and out into a pitch-dark alley.

A two-horse buckboard had the back seat taken out, making room for the litter which they slid into the bed of it. "Slap a tarp over him, Jody, and let's get to hell outa here."

When the tarp was in place, Murph whipped the team to a trot, Jody sitting in the wagon bed with the canvas-covered prisoner. "We can be a mile away by the time she gets back with the doc," Murph calculated.

They came out of the alley and turned west to Garden, where there were no saloons or lights. Murph kept to dark streets, finally doubling back east, and presently was free of the town.

V

Douglas Madigan, wearing waders, fly fished on McKay Creek, long enough to be seen by two passersby. At both contacts Madigan complained that the trout weren't striking. "If they don't start hitting soon I'll ride over and try East Birch."

His switch to East Birch would now seem to be an afterthought. Madigan arrived there in early afternoon, tying his horse in creek-bank brush just below the Costain house. Again he rigged up his fly-rod and fished for an hour, creeling a dozen native trout.

By then he'd spotted the place where Durwin had dug day before yesterday. For Madigan this wasn't too difficult, since he himself had selected the spot two summers ago. Then he leaned his rod against a tree, ready to use it again if someone should come along. He walked to the Costain barn and found the old irrigation shovel. Fresh clay clinging to the blade confirmed its recent use by Durwin.

Not that Madigan had doubted Durwin's statement. The key to Post Office Box 60 had been more than convincing. Missing it two years ago, a day after his crime on East Birch Creek, Madigan supposed he'd mislaid it somewhere. Postmaster Livermore had furnished him with a duplicate key and Madigan had thought no more about it.

At the burial spot he soon had the trench open again. The first thing he took out was the jug of whiskey. He poured the liquor into the creek, then with a heavy rock he smashed the jug into bits.

One by one he threw the fragments into the stream.

Next he took out the three rusty rifles and the two skinning knives. These he put in a grain sack brought along for the purpose. He wrapped his rain slicker around the sack and tied all of it back of the cantle of his saddle.

Then came the hard, slow part—retrieving more than fifty brass cartridges. Mixed with dirt and clay there, one or two of them would be easy to overlook. If the sheriff found even one cartridge it could be enough to verify Durwin's story.

He had to assume that Durwin would ultimately recover his wits and tell what he'd found here. Accused, Madigan would steadfastly deny it. Which would leave the word of a stranger against the word of a popular citizen. The sheriff, guided by Durwin, would of course check here. Nor could Madigan forget that a doctor named McKay had from the first maintained that a white man or men, not Indians, had raided the Costains.

At last he was able to backfill the hole and return his shovel to the barn. He unjointed the fly-rod and tied it on his saddle, atop the bulky, slicker-wrapped grain sack. With a creel of trout hanging from his saddle horn, he mounted and rode toward Pendleton.

It was a cloudy, moonless night. He couldn't feel safe until the rifles and the knives were disposed of.

A good place would be the Umatilla River two or three miles below Pendleton. Madigan rode slowly that way, through darkness, his mind brooding over the misstep which had plunged him into the Costain crime.

The specialty of his law practice was probate work and estate management. The biggest plum which had come his way was the Glenn Hollister estate—one of the largest in Umatilla County. It included a cattle ranch on Meadow Creek, a sheep ranch on Butter Creek, a brick business block on Main Street in Pendleton, and half a dozen parcels of town rental property. For health reasons Glenn Hollister had gone back to his home in Tennessee three years ago, yet with such confidence that property values in Oregon would increase that he'd elected not to sell out. He'd retained Douglas Madigan to keep the properties leased, collect rents, and make quarterly reports. Only once had he sent an auditor to check on Madigan's stewardship.

That was two years ago, just after Madigan had gambled away eight thousand dollars of Hollister money at the Walla Walla Club, Max Charny's card and dice resort on Cottonwood Street. With an auditor on the way to Pendleton, Madigan had faced exposure and a prison term unless he could cover the shortage before the man's arrival. In desperation he'd ridden to the Costain ranch hoping to borrow money the brothers had just taken in on a cattle sale.

They'd been cordial—but their answer had been no. With Indians raiding and ravaging not more than twenty miles away, Madigan had played raider himself. With the Costain money he'd covered up his shortage at Pendleton.

Now, after two years, he was still managing the Hollister estate. Land values had doubled and the estate had prospered. So had Doug Madigan's practice. He was local attorney for the Wells-Fargo Express Company and for the John Hailey Stagecoach Line. Fees and commissions had made Madigan comfortably affluent, and in another few years would make him rich.

Now, out of the clear sky, came Kent Durwin! Durwin with his story of digging up rifles, knives, bullets, a whiskey jug, and the key to Post Office Box 60!

Subconsciously Madigan had feared something like that from the first. It was why, after being directed by the niece in Michigan to sell the Costain ranch, he'd purposely delayed the sale by fixing a high price with the terms all cash.

He hadn't wanted a ranch family moving into that bullet-pitted cabin too soon, lest they should stumble onto some overlooked clue. To convince the Michigan heir that he was trying, he'd occasionally advertised the property and sent her a copy of the ad. Finally an ad in a Denver paper had brought Kent Durwin.

In a few days Durwin was sure to regain his wits and tell a tale on Madigan. If people believed it, the lawyer's whole world would come tumbling down. An important part of that world was Nancy Rollins. She hadn't said yes yet; but neither had she said no.

It was nearly midnight when Madigan heard the roar of the Umatilla River in the darkness ahead. He struck it at the mouth of McKay Creek and lost no time taking the slicker-wrapped grain sack from his saddle.

Madigan threw one of the rifles as far as he could into the river. Then he walked up the bank, leading his horse. One by one he got rid of the other rifles and the skinning knives, throwing them into the rapids at intervals of about a quarter mile. The cartridges he threw in by the handful.

Mounting, Madigan rode on into Pendleton. No one saw him turn in at a cottage at the corner of Willow and Webb. He put his horse in a shed back of it. This minor residence property was part of the Hollister estate and Madigan used it as a bachelor apartment, generally taking his noon and evening meals at the Villard House. Normally he kept his riding horse at a livery stable; but tonight his late return from a fishing trip might seem a bit unnatural. By avoiding a public stable, he could claim to have arrived home shortly after dark.

He took his creel of trout into the cottage by the back door. In the morning he could dress the fish and give them to Nancy and her friend Amy.

Now to bed. He was taking off his boots when he heard riders gallop by along Willow. He opened a window in time to see the silhouettes of five mounted men wheel from Willow into Webb Street. In the darkness he couldn't recognize them but the shouting voice of the leader seemed to be Sheriff Martin's.

Was it a posse of some kind? Hardly a week passed without a shooting affair at one of the Pendleton saloons. There could have been one tonight.

Madigan sat down and took off the other boot. More sounds came to him through the open window. Two loud-talking men were passing, perhaps on their way home after a carousal.

With a shock Madigan heard a name spoken. The name *Durwin!* Instantly he was alert and fearful.

Could it mean that Durwin had regained his wits and had told a tale? A tale about murder at midnight on a bridge?

No, because in that case Sheriff Martin would have knocked on this door instead of riding by. Nor would the sheriff need a five-man posse to question someone accused by Durwin.

Yet something sensational must have taken place tonight—something which involved Durwin. What else could involve Durwin other than his findings at the Costain ranch?

Madigan continued to undress, but only to change from his fishing clothes. He put on a town suit and hurried out to the street. He walked east along Webb to Main and turned in at Mattlock's Webfoot Saloon. The bar was full and there was noisy talk. Talk about Kent Durwin!

Madigan ordered a whiskey, his lips sealed and his ears wide open.

"Did the Olsen woman recognize 'em?" a man asked.

The bartender had an answer. "Didn't get a very good look at 'em, she says. Lamp had a shade over it and the light was dim; one guy claimed the other guy was shot and he sure looked like it. Other fella said he'd put him to bed while the Olsen woman was fetchin' a doctor."

"How long was she gone, Eb?"

"Not more'n twenty-thirty minutes. Time she got back with Doc McKay the place was plumb empty."

"You mean they fooled her?"

"They sure did. Seems those two jaspers just

picked up the Durwin boy and walked out with him."

"Why the heck would they do that, Eb?"

Eb, the bartender, shrugged. "I ain't got the faintest idea, Mack. Neither has the sheriff or Doc McKay."

VI

Early in the morning Madigan took his riding horse to a Main Street livery stable, lingering there to listen in on talk about last night's sensation. A downriver stock hand was saddling up after a night on the town. "They got any idea who did it?" he asked.

"Sure they have, Matt. Who else but the same bozo who chucked him off the bridge. Him and some pal of his. Had to get him out of there before he came to and snitched on 'em. Maybe they tossed him back into the river. Or maybe they just hauled him off to some gully and slit his throat."

No one around the livery barn had a better idea than that. Madigan went back to the Willow Street cottage, cleaned his catch of trout, and fried two of them. The rest he made into a package which he took along when he started to his office.

He was passing a large two-story residence when its occupant came out and hailed him. "Wait a minute, Doug. It'll save me a trip to your office. It's rent day, remember? Here you are."

The man handed Madigan a check for sixty-five dollars, drawn on a Portland bank.

"Thanks, Judge." Madigan pocketed the check. He'd leased this house, which was a parcel of the Hollister estate, to Judge William LaDow of the Umatilla County Court. The Hollisters had used it as a town house, a place to stay whenever shopping or social errands had brought them in from their Meadow Creek ranch. It was one of the few pretentious residences of Pendleton, with tall, shuttered windows. Here at the street was a quarried carriage block so that a lady with a ground-length skirt could more easily step into or out of a surrey or buggy; also a cast-iron hitching post. Glenn Hollister, born and raised on a Tennessee plantation, had brought his tastes and traditions along with him to Oregon.

"What's this I hear about a kidnapping last night, Doug?" the judge asked.

"Don't know a thing about it, Judge." It was an answer Madigan could give with sincerity.

He scribbled a receipt for a month's rent and handed it to LaDow.

"What about the note this Durwin boy slipped under McKay's door?"

Madigan shrugged. "Can't figure it. They say it was something about McKay being right and everybody else wrong."

"Only thing that fits that," the judge reasoned, "is the Costain massacre two years ago."

"Seems like it. Well, so long, Judge. See you in court."

Madigan moved a block east down Alta Street to the Garden Street corner and knocked at a cottage door. Amy Brundage opened it. "You're too late, Mr. Madigan," she told him. "Nancy has already gone to her office."

"Just stopped by to drop these off." Madigan handed her the package of trout.

Before he reached the Hollister Block stairs he was button-holed several times. "Slept right through it," he told everyone.

At the top of the stairs he heard voices from Doctor McKay's private office.

One was Sheriff Martin's. "Must've been hauled off in a wagon of some kind, Doctor. But the town was full of wagons last night. No one noticed which ones pulled out about midnight. Dark as pitch. Two men with beards, you say, Mrs. Olsen?"

Madigan could easily recognize Mrs. Olsen's Swedish accent. "Yes sir. Hairy faces and they had droopy hat brims. My lamp was turned low and I couldn't see them very well. One man was tall; the other looked short but maybe it was because his knees were bent. Red on his shirt looked like blood . . ."

"Blood made of catsup, I'll wager," offered Doctor McKay.

The sheriff gave a growl of agreement. "I checked and there was no gunplay at the Webfoot Bar last night."

The next words came from Nancy Rollins in a tone of remorse. "We should have kept a guard over him. They tried to kill him on the bridge; so we might have known they'd try again."

McKay spoke up shrewdly. "I don't think it was the same people. Whoever attacked him on the bridge clearly meant to kill him. But last night's kidnappers didn't. It would have been easy for them to garrott him in bed. Instead they took him away alive, which was risky. It's more like they need him for a hostage, or pawn, for one purpose or another."

Madigan unlocked his own office and went in. He raised a window blind and stood staring out at the Main Street crowds. Across at the courthouse clusters of men stood in the courtyard, no doubt waiting for the latest report on the abduction of Kent Durwin.

At his desk Madigan tried to pin his mind on a court case coming up tomorrow. It had been scheduled for yesterday but he'd contrived a postponement—a delay which had enabled him to get rid of the infernal Costain rifles.

It meant that he'd missed picking up yesterday's mail. No use trying to work with his nerves jumping like this; so Madigan went down to the street and to the post office on the Water Street corner. From there it was less than forty paces to the bridge where he'd lured Durwin.

In the post office he took a key from his pocket—a key whose brass tag had the number *60*. In Box 60 he found accumulated mail. The most important letter was one postmarked Knoxville, Tennessee. It was from his client Glenn Hollister. The last paragraph was:

> We will continue our policy of leasing instead of selling, at least until the railroad gets there. My information is that the Union Pacific is now building a branch to be called the Oregon Short Line which will cross southern Idaho and eventually pass through Pendleton on its way to Portland. When that happens (probably no later than the summer of 1882) the value of my properties in your capable hands should be substantially enhanced.

Madigan went back to his office. At noon he crossed the hall hoping to persuade Nancy Rollins to take lunch with him. She wasn't at her desk. A patient waiting there explained, "The sheriff just called her and Doctor McKay over to the courthouse."

"What for?" Madigan asked nervously.

The man shrugged. "*Quien sabe?*"

Why would Sheriff Martin call them to the courthouse? Had Durwin been found?

Madigan lunched alone at the Villard House. On the way out he spoke to Lot Livermore, who usually knew more about Pendleton affairs than anyone else. But today the postmaster was as mystified as was Madigan himself. "It just don't make sense, Doug."

The best listening post in town, usually, was Max Charny's Walla Walla Club on Cottonwood Street. The games there didn't begin till three o'clock but the bar would be open now. Madigan went directly there from the hotel.

Only a dozen customers were in the place. No house play was on but two ranchers were playing high card for a dollar a cut. Charny wasn't in sight but his fascinating red-haired hostess sat alone at an end of the bar, nibbling a sandwich and sipping coffee. She was a slender young woman with pearl earrings, quiet and even formal in her greetings to the guests, never overdressed or over rouged. Some suspected that she was Charny's wife posing as a single woman in order to better charm the patrons. More than a few Pendleton men were in love with her and most of the Pendleton housewives resented her. As Madigan passed her she gave him a pleasant nod. "Good afternoon, Mr. Madigan."

Madigan bought a beer and carried it to a table, where he joined a popular Main Street merchant named Switzer.

"Hi, Doug. Hear any more about what happened to young Durwin?"

"Not a word, Charlie."

"Wonder if Helena knows anything," Switzer pondered. His gaze was on the red-haired hostess.

"Maybe we ought to call her over here and buy her a drink."

The idea didn't appeal to Madigan. He preferred not to appear too curious about Durwin. "Let's leave her alone, Charlie. She wouldn't know anything."

"How long has she been with Charny? More than two years, isn't it?"

Madigan thought back. "She came here in seventy-seven," he remembered. "Seems to me it was right after the gunfight down on the Glenn Hollister ranch. When the Hollister boy shot it out with a Kansas outlaw."

"You're right, Doug." It had been the sensation of the season, Roy Hollister killing and being killed. An even-break draw-fight in a ranch corral. Roy had lived less than a minute after the smoke cleared; but the Kansan who'd sought him out and provoked the showdown had lived an hour—long enough to proclaim with profane bitterness that Roy Hollister was a "dirty double-crosser."

"Broke his old man's heart," Charlie Switzer remembered. "Roy comin' to a bad end like that. Everybody knew Roy was a wild one; but that outlaw from Kansas showin' up with a gun was the first we knew of Roy playing around with his kind. Broke his dad's heart and I reckon that's the reason he leased out the ranch and went back to Tennessee."

Madigan nodded absently, his eyes on Max Charny, who'd just come out of his private office and was heading this way. The gambling proprietor was short and wide, with a wine-red complexion and thick tawny hair parted in the middle. Always he wore a tailormade gray suit with a gold watch chain spanning his vest.

He came to Douglas Madigan and spoke quietly. "What about an appointment at nine tomorrow morning, Doug? At your office. Got a little matter coming up and I need your advice."

"I have to be in court at ten," Madigan told him.

"That's all right, Doug. My business won't take more 'n a few minutes. You can still be in court at ten."

"Okay," Madigan agreed. "In my office at nine tomorrow morning."

The lawyer left the Walla Walla Club and was heading for his office when Ed Pitcher, a freighter, came out of a billiard hall and hailed him. "What was the idea of postponing my case?" he complained. "It was supposed to be yesterday."

"Sorry, Ed. I needed some rest so I took a day off and went fishing. It's now set for ten o'clock tomorrow. See you in court."

In his office Madigan reviewed the case, which was fairly simple. Ed Pitcher was suing the Maverick Saloon to recover six hundred dollars, claiming the barkeeper there had given him a knockout drop and then rolled him; and that he'd come to his senses six hundred dollars poorer. Two witnesses had seen the victim kicked unconscious out the alley door. Things like that had happened before at the Maverick, which was the toughest saloon in town.

With two eye-witnesses, the suit should be easy to win.

At six o'clock Madigan picked up Nancy Rollins and took her to dinner at the Villard House. Not once did Nancy mention Kent Durwin. But she was preoccupied and Madigan had an idea her mind was on Durwin. When he took her home she didn't ask him to come in.

He was at his desk at nine in the morning and Max Charny appeared only a minute later. "I won't keep you long, Doug. Just want to trade favors with you. You do one for me, I do one for you."

Two things alarmed Madigan. Before coming in Charny had looked cautiously both ways along the hall. Then he'd closed the door, drawn up a chair so that he could sit knee to knee with the lawyer, and was speaking in a guarded voice.

"What favor," Madigan probed uneasily, "would you want me to do for you?"

"The lease on the Hollister cow ranch expires next week," Charny reminded him. "The outgoing tenant, Pete Carter, doesn't want to renew. He's moving to his own place on the John Day River."

Madigan nodded. More than a month ago Carter had given notice that he didn't intend to renew his lease.

"So you'll need a new tenant, Doug. What about letting Sol Olcutt move in there for the next year? Same terms as you gave Carter."

Madigan could hardly believe he'd heard rightly. Olcutt was no stockman. He was Charny's second in command at the Walla Walla gambling club here in Pendleton.

"What the devil does Olcutt know about a cow ranch? Anyway you're too late. Glenn Hollister is sending a nephew of his out to try his hand at running that ranch. Young fella named Landers and he's on his way here now. Due in a week from today on the Hailey stage."

Charny frowned. "You can tell him you've already rented the place, can't you?"

"No. Because I've acknowledged Mr. Hollister's instruction and said I'd hold the place for his nephew."

The gambling man sat brooding for a moment. "A tenderfoot from Tennessee, huh? We'll have to figure out a way to discourage him; get him to change his mind and go back home."

"Look, Charny," Madigan said sharply. "Why should I turn down my client's nephew to lease a big cattle ranch to a card-and-dice man like Olcutt?"

"Because I'll square it up, Doug, by doing an even bigger favor for you."

A sly narrowing of the man's eyes brought a chill to Madigan. He tried to speak calmly. "I'm listening. What favor could you do for me?"

Charny leaned forward and explained quietly. "A few nights ago I was taking a cup of coffee at the St. Louis Restaurant. You know where it is—on the east side of Main just short of Water Street. I had a table by the front window and I saw two men pass on the far walk, moving north toward the bridge. It was midnight and plenty dark, but one of the men lighted a cigarette and I could see by the flare he was you."

Madigan waited, braced for the worst. His heart thumped as Charny went on, "The two men disappeared in the dark toward the bridge. Three minutes later one of them came walking back south, alone. It was you, Madigan, who hit Durwin on the head and dropped him off the bridge."

"You can't prove it."

"No," Charny admitted, "*But Durwin can.* All I have to do is turn him loose." Slyly the gambler added, "He can tell where he was that day and why he left a note at McKay's office saying the doctor was right. It's a safe bet he can tell why you steered him to the bridge and got rid of him."

"You mean you . . ." Madigan choked on his question and by the look on Charny's wine-streaked face he knew he didn't need to ask it.

"That's right," the man assured him bluntly. "I mean the two men who packed him away from here are working for me. They'll do what I say. They'll hold Durwin safe where he is as long as you figure a way to give Sol Olcutt that ranch lease. They've got him a far piece from here and you could never find the place. If you even try to find it we'll turn the boy loose and let him head for the sheriff."

"And if I do get you that lease, what then?"

"Then we'll tell you where Durwin is. You can go to him, if you like, and finish the dirty work you started on the bridge."

"You wouldn't dare turn him loose," Madigan argued hoarsely. "He'd tell a tale on *you,* too. And there'd be two of us on our way to Salem." The Oregon state prison was at Salem.

Max Charny smiled and shook his head. "Not me. You'd land at Salem but not me. Durwin never heard of me and his two guards won't mention my name. He'll tell on *them,* naturally, if he gets a chance. But by the time he gets to the law they'll be where the law can't find them."

The gambler stood up and moved to the door. There he turned with an afterthought. "One other thing I want you to do for me, Doug. You postponed your case against the Maverick

Saloon. It's set for ten this morning. I want you to postpone it again."

Madigan gaped at him. "Postpone it again? Why?"

"To give your two witnesses time to get out of Oregon. I'll see that they've got stage and boat fare. Without 'em you can't win that suit, right?"

The lawyer gave a baffled nod. His entire case against the Maverick Bar depended on those eye-witnesses.

Charny read the puzzlement in Madigan's eyes and explained frankly. "I'll let you in on a little secret, Doug. I *own* the Maverick. Got the title in someone else's name but it's my property, just like the Walla Walla Club. We've got two kinds of suckers in this town," he confided. "The high flyers who like plush trimmings; and the sheepherders and the bullwhackers and cowboys and miners who shy away from plush trimmings. That class of trade goes to the Maverick and we know just how to trim 'em." Charny lowered an eyelid. "The same thing happens at the Walla Walla, only we've got smoother methods there."

"And where," Madigan asked with a vacant stare, "does a ranch lease come in?" The holding of Durwin at some hideout made sense; but leasing a cattle ranch to Sol Olcutt didn't.

"Some day," Charny promised, "I'll let you

in on it. Right now you'd better go over to the courthouse and wangle a postponement. Then you can start figuring a way to discourage that nephew from Tennessee."

VII

Salisbury, Hailey and Company's overland stage, rolling northwest toward its breakfast stop at Meacham, had for the last hour been climbing a gentle grade through the Blue Mountains. Tall pines lining the trail shut off the rising sun. As the grade steepened driver Jack Wyatt let his six-in-hand slow to a walk. Inside the big Concord coach all but three of his eight passengers were still asleep. There'd been eleven drivers, and thirty-six changes of horses, since the beginning of this run at Kelton, Utah, where the stage line connected with the Union Pacific Railroad.

The three wide-awake passengers shared the rearmost of the coach's three seats. Donna Costain, sitting between a young man named Tony Landers and a grizzled old-timer named Josh Bixby, had become so trail-weary at Boise City, Idaho, that she'd laid over there a day for rest. Tony Landers had come straight through from Kelton; and Bixby had boarded at the last change stop: LaGrande, Oregon.

"We'll get an A-one breakfast at Meacham," the old-timer promised his seatmates.

"How many more stops after that," Donna asked wearily, "before we get to Pendleton?"

"Only two. Pelican and Cayuse. We'll fetch

up at the Villard House at Pendleton in time for supper."

"Does this coach go any further than that?" Tony Landers wondered.

"Yep. Forty-odd miles further to Umatilla Landing on the Columbia River. Connects there with a riverboat if you want to go on to Portland."

"You said you knew my uncle, Glenn Hollister?"

"Knowed him well. Stopped overnight at his Meadow Creek ranch more 'n once, when I was down that way after elk."

Although they'd only known him since the LaGrande stop, the others were aware by now that Josh Bixby was an ex-hunter, an ex-bullwhacker, an ex-bartender, and an ex-Indian-fighter who'd spent most of the last fourteen years in and around Pendleton.

"Do you know Jerry DeSpain?" Tony asked him.

"Who doesn't? Biggest stockman in the country, Jerry is. Why?"

"My Uncle Glenn gave me a letter of introduction to him; so I can ask him to recommend an experienced ranch hand. This'll be my first try at running a cattle ranch and I'll need some expert help."

"Sure you will," Bixby agreed. "And you can depend on anyone Jerry DeSpain steers your way."

The trail leveled off and driver Wyatt again whipped his horses to a trot. The jolt wakened the Horace Mumfords in the middle seat. The woman rubbed her eyes and then turned with a question. "Where are we, Mr. Bixby?"

"Only a half mile short of breakfast, ma'am."

The three passengers on the front seat were still drowsing.

Donna asked, "Do you know a Pendleton lawyer named Madigan?"

"Doug Madigan? Everybody knows Doug," Bixby said. "Got his finger in every pie, Doug has. Biggest practice in east Oregon."

The name alerted Tony Landers. He turned curiously toward Donna Costain. "You mean you've got business with Madigan? So have I. He handles my Uncle Glenn's Oregon properties. My uncle wrote him that I'm on my way to take over the Meadow Creek cattle ranch."

"I wonder how far," Donna said, "your ranch is from mine. Mine's on East Birch Creek and all I know about it is that it's been vacant for two years. I told Mr. Madigan to sell it but so far he hasn't found a buyer. Do you know the place, Mr. Bixby?"

"Look, Miss," the old-timer said, "there ain't a corner in the county I don't know. I packed a rifle in that volunteer militia two years ago when we smacked down on them Bannocks. If we'd done it a month sooner the Costain boys'd still be alive. Come to think of it, I heard they had a niece in Michigan; only kin they had. That you, Miss?"

Donna nodded. She was a small, blue-eyed girl with braids of yellow hair coiled under her traveling bonnet. "I can't remember my uncles very well; I was only a child when they left home."

"They're buried in the Pilot Rock graveyard," Bixby told her. "Lawyer Madigan sold their livestock. Everything but the house and land."

"I have to pay taxes on it," the girl said, "and it doesn't seem right to let it stand vacant. I've always wanted to go west. My grandfather went west to Michigan and my uncles went west to Oregon. So now it's my turn and I want to find out why my agent can't sell what everyone says is a perfectly good ranch."

The coach stopped abruptly with a rasp of brakes. Tony looked out and saw a two-story log house with sheds and corrals back of it. At the house door an Indian boy was beating on a tin pan. From the driver's seat Jack Wyatt shouted, "We're at Meacham, folks. All out for breakfast. You got thirty minutes while we hook up fresh horses."

Tony helped Donna out of the coach. Then a lanky, leatherclad man came out of the house picking his teeth. A badge on his jacket announced that he was a deputy sheriff of Umatilla County.

Wyatt hailed him. "Hi, Andy. What you doin' this far from the courthouse? Chasin' horse thieves?"

"Nope, Jack," the deputy said. "I'm out huntin' a coupla kidnappers. Bob Sargent's scoutin' down the Umatilla Landing road and Sperry's scoutin' up toward Walla Walla. We're after a coupla rough lookers with droopy black hats, both bearded, one tall, one short, drivin' a buckboard or spring wagon."

"Haven't seen anyone like that, Andy."

"This is as far as I'm supposed to go," Andy said. "Soon as I grain my horse I'll head back toward Pendleton."

Breakfast was ham, scrambled eggs, fried potatoes, and coffee. Donna sat beside Mrs. Horace Mumford, a middle-aged woman who seemed nervous, half-frightened, as if she might be thinking of hostile Indians or stage robbers. She and her husband had come all the way from Kelton on this coach and had generally kept to themselves.

Deputy Andy McDowd, who'd already breakfasted, sat by the stove and answered questions from Bixby and Wyatt.

"Young fella named Durwin got conked on the bean and tossed in the river. He washed ashore at a bend and they took him half dead to Doc McKay's ward. Coupla night later two toughies snatched him outa bed and vamoosed with him."

The name Durwin was strange to everyone at

the table. "Newcomer in town?" Wyatt asked.

"Yep. Came in from Colorado figurin' to buy himself a ranch and start raisin' beef."

A hostler came in to announce that fresh horses were now traced to the stage. "Next stop, Pelican," Wyatt said as he herded his passengers outside.

As they reboarded the coach a saddled horse was led from a corral and delivered to Deputy McDowd. The saddle had a scabbard with a carbine slanting upward from it. Wyatt whipped his six-in-hand to a trot and the stage rolled on northwesterly through a forest of fir and pine.

Donna, Tony, and Bixby again had the rear three seats. Looking back, Donna saw Deputy McDowd following them at a running walk. A minute later she looked back again and failed to see him. "Why can't he keep up?" the girl asked Bixby.

"Because our hosses can run and his can't. We change hosses every two or three hours but he has to ride the same one all the way to Pendleton. Means he has to take it easy."

A doe with fawn by her side ran across the trail. Wyatt let his horses walk for a while, then whipped them to a run again.

Bixby, Tony remembered, had mentioned being out after elk several times when he'd stopped overnight at the Glenn Hollister ranch. "Lots of game down that way?" he asked.

"More than you can shake a stick at," Bixby told him. "Elk, deer, black bear, ducks, prairie chickens. That's why those six Union soldiers staked out that land in the first place."

"Union soldiers? What about them?"

"When the war was over, six vets from General Grant's army hit the Oregon Trail with a couple of covered wagons and didn't stop till they got to Umatilla County. They went down to Meadow Crik and each of 'em homesteaded a quarter section. They'd each been issued soldier's script, which entitled each man to buy another quarter section for a dollar two-bits an acre. Later they bought an adjoinin' school section, which made in all a four-section ranch."

"How long did they stay there?" Tony asked.

"Until about eighteen seventy-four, when your uncle came along and bought 'em out. He had great faith in this country, your uncle did. Built himself a fancy town house in Pendleton and put up a brick block on Main Street."

"If he liked Oregon so well," Donna wondered, "why did he leave?"

"Said it was for his health. But most folks figger it was on account of his boy Roy. Roy was a wild one and away from home most of the time. In the spring of seventy-seven he came home and a bad actor from Kansas followed him to the Meadow Crik ranch. They cut loose at each other, bullet for bullet. It left two dead men there in the Hollister corral and Glenn never got over it. Purty soon he leased the ranch to Pete Carter and moved back to Tennessee."

The look on Tony's face made Donna sorry she'd asked her question. It had served only to drag out a family skeleton. To change the subject she asked, "How long will we be in this forest, Mr. Bixby?"

"Not long, Miss. Purty soon we top a little divide they call Dead Man's Pass. Beyond that we're mostly in the open and the grade's downhill all the way to Pendleton."

Wyatt was walking his team on an upgrade. Everything to the west of them, Bixby explained, was in the Umatilla Indian Reservation. To the east the wooded Blue Mountains reached almost to the Snake River on the Idaho line.

"Another half mile and we'll be at the pass."

Josh Bixby had no more than spoken when the coach came to an abrupt halt. Tony looked out and saw two mounted men each wearing a mask and aiming a rifle at driver Wyatt.

"Throw down the box," one of them commanded.

The other man shouted, "Everybody out on this side and line up."

"It's a holdup," Bixby whispered. "Don't fool with them fellas. Just do like they say."

Tony took out his wallet and slipped it under the seat leather. He looked out and saw a padlocked box hit the ground. Wyatt's shotgun followed it; then the driver himself climbed down with his hands raised.

One by one the eight passengers got out. As they lined up, Tony remembered Deputy McDowd. McDowd couldn't be more than a mile or so behind them.

One of the robbers sat his saddle and kept his rifle aimed at Wyatt, who himself now stood unarmed in the line. The other robber dismounted with a grain sack in hand. He moved along the line taking wallets, watches, and pocket money from the men, and a purse from Donna Costain. He found nothing on either of the Mumfords. Yet clearly the Mumfords were more frightened than anyone else.

The mounted robber snapped a reminder to his partner. "Look inside and see if they ditched anything."

He kept his rifle at an aim while the other masked man was searching the coach. When the man came out he had three wallets. Tony saw that one of them was his own. The others probably belonged to the hardware salesman and Mumford.

The man dropped his take into the grain sack. He picked up the Wells-Fargo express box and dropped it into the same sack. He tied the sack back of his cantle and was preparing to mount when the other robber again snapped a reminder.

"You forgot somethin', didn'tja?" His eyes were fixed on Tony Landers.

The unmounted man nodded, then walked to Tony and hit him hard on the head with the barrel of a gun. It staggered Tony. He reeled against the coach but managed to keep his feet.

His next awareness was of a shot being fired from down the trail. He looked dizzily that way and saw Andy McDowd. The deputy was standing by his horse and had the stock of a carbine at his cheek. He fired again—and three times at a range of not more than a hundred yards. His third shot found its target and the outlaw in the act of mounting fell sideways to the ground. His horse snorted, ran a few steps, then stopped as it stepped on a dangling rein.

The robber who'd kept his saddle wheeled his mount and was off at a hard run into the timber.

Through it all the Mumford woman had stood panic-stricken in the line. Now from sheer relief she fainted. The sudden awkward fall left the woman's outer skirt rumpled in a fold which exposed her sateen underskirt from ankles to knees.

Donna Costain, who'd stood next to her in the line, saw the woman's husband stoop quickly and smooth the dress down again.

Vaguely it made Donna aware that her brief glimpse of the underskirt had given the impression of bulky lumps or padding. Was something of value hidden in the hem or lining of that sateen undergarment? It would explain why the Mumfords, all through this stage journey, had seemed nervously on edge.

Then Deputy McDowd came riding up and Donna forgot all about the Mumfords. McDowd dismounted and stooped briefly over the fallen robber. "Dead," he reported. From the man's saddle he took the loot sack and dumped the contents on the ground.

"Everybody can pick out his own stuff," he invited.

Then he saw Tony Landers leaning dizzily against the coach with blood trickling from a head cut. "Cracked down on you, did he?" the deputy suggested. "Maybe you tried to hold out on him."

Tony admitted it with a nod.

"Somethin' funny 'bout it," Josh Bixby said. "Three of us tried to hold out on him. But the only one he whanged down on was Landers. Didn't even do that till his pard reminded him. 'You forgot somethin', didn'tja?' the other fella said; and he looked straight at Landers. Like whangin' him over the head was unfinished business. Did anybody know you'd be on this coach, boy?"

Tony was too groggy to answer. Only later did he remember that he'd written the Hollister estate agent, Douglas Madigan, that he'd arrive in Pendleton on Wednesday evening. Today was Wednesday.

VIII

The daily arrival of a stagecoach from a Utah railhead five hundred miles away was always an event in Pendleton. Its first stop was at the Villard House and on this summer evening a score of citizens were there to see the coach roll in. One of them was Sheriff Bill Martin and another was Douglas Madigan.

As usual, Jack Wyatt made it a point to arrive at a gallop and then brake to a sudden wheel-skidding stop at the hotel's Court Street entrance. He was glad to see Sheriff Martin there because he had big news to tell. "We got stuck up," he announced, "a piece this side of Meacham. They didn't get nothin', though. Andy McDowd rid up and gunned 'em down."

This was the first word of it to reach Pendleton. There was a telegraph line west to Portland but as yet there was no wire service east. Stagecoach trouble in the Blue Mountains could be reported only by the stage itself.

"Anybody get hurt, Jack?"

"Yep. Andy beaned one of the robbers and we left him at Pelican dead as a coffin nail. But not before the fella whanged one of my passengers over the head. How you feelin', boy?"

Passengers were getting out of the coach and one of them was a young stranger with a freshly bandaged scalp. He grinned at the driver. "I'm okay—except you just about rattled my teeth out coming down that grade."

He turned to help a girl out of the stage. She too was a stranger—a small, delicate blonde wearing a blue traveling cape with bonnet to match. Her eyes too were blue as they looked about with vivid excitement at this new world to which she'd come after a long, tedious journey by rail and stagecoach.

The Horace Mumfords were the first to go inside. Wyatt was now down from the driver's seat and was taking bags from the baggage boot. A hotel porter put the bags in a pushcart and went inside with them.

All this while Sheriff Martin was firing questions. "You say McDowd killed one bandit and the other got away? Any idea who they were?"

"We know who the dead man was," Wyatt told him. "When we took his mask off we could see he was Cass Clardy who usta tend bar at the Maverick Saloon. What we can't figure out is—why did he crack down on Landers? Didn't touch anybody else, just young Landers. Landers hadn't talked back to him, or anything. It was kinda like part of the holdup job was to smack the boy down."

Douglas Madigan, on the rear edge of the crowd, changed his mind about pressing forward to introduce himself to Tony Landers. The news about a holdup startled him. Had Max Charny pulled the strings for it? Since one of the holdup men was a tough from the Maverick Saloon, quite likely the other one was too; and Madigan now knew that Charny owned the Maverick.

He watched Tony Landers and the girl follow their baggage into the lobby. He had no idea who the girl was. The girl was given a second-floor room and Landers a room on the ground floor. Probably they were just casual stagecoach acquaintances.

Madigan sat in a lobby chair, lighted a cigarette and pinned his mind on Max Charny. Charny, who wanted to discourage Landers from taking over the lease of the Hollister ranch. If he were a timid sort, being batted down by stagecoach robbers might make him wish he'd stayed in Tennessee. For the past year there'd been an organized gang of outlaws operating in eastern Oregon, driving off livestock, holding up stages, ambushing payrolls and Wells-Fargo shipments. Till now, it hadn't occurred to Madigan that the brains behind that gang might be Charny.

Yet clearly Charny had outlaws at his beck and call. A pair of them had kidnapped Kent Durwin for the purpose of forcing Madigan to obey Charny's orders. Another pair connected with Charny's underworld saloon had held up a stagecoach with the double object of robbing it and wantonly assaulting one of its passengers.

Under pressure from Charny, Madigan had already arranged a second postponement of Ed Pitcher's lawsuit against the Maverick Saloon. But more important to Charny was the lease on Glenn Hollister's Meadow Creek ranch. He wanted it given to Sol Olcutt instead of to the owner's nephew.

Why, Madigan wondered, did Charny and Olcutt want that ranch lease? They were cards-and-dice men, not stock-growers.

Presently he went to the lobby desk for a look at the registry book. He was mildly curious about the girl who'd just signed her name there. Now he learned that she was Donna Costain and that she'd come from Lansing, Michigan.

So here was another of his clients! One who two years ago had instructed him to sell her property on East Birch Creek. Why hadn't she notified him that she was coming?

Madigan went into the barroom and bought himself a drink. It was the supper hour and people were converging on the dining room. Tony Landers appeared and stood looking up the stairs in an attitude of expectant waiting.

Then Donna Costain came down and joined him. Her yellow dinner dress matched the corn-colored hair which was wound in a coil at the back of her head. Tony took her into the dining room. Evidently they'd arranged it while still riding on the stage. Madigan concluded that they'd become better than just casual stagecoach acquaintances. The boy might even be in love with the girl. In that case talking him into changing his plans would be harder than ever.

To whom should he talk first, the boy or the girl?

Madigan still hadn't made up his mind when they finished dinner and came out into the lobby. He saw them say good night to each other, the girl going up to her second-floor room and Landers disappearing rearward down a ground-floor corridor.

He'd see Landers right now, the lawyer decided, and call on the girl tomorrow. According to the registry book, Landers had Room 108. Madigan went to it and knocked. When the door opened he went in briskly, talking fast.

"You're Glenn Hollister's nephew? Good! Welcome to Oregon. I'm Doug Madigan; been handling your uncle's affairs ever since he left here. What's this I hear about some highwayman socking you on the head?"

Tony grinned and shook hands. "Reckon the fella didn't like me; acted kinda like he knew I'd be on that stage and was layin' for me."

"That's funny!" Madigan's hearty smile changed to a frown of puzzlement. "But wait a minute. Lots of people could know you were coming in on Wednesday's coach. It was in the Pendleton paper couple of days ago. Gave it out myself as a news item. Sorry."

Tony shrugged. "Doesn't matter; all I got was a headache. By the way, Mr. Madigan, you won't need to use your power-of-attorney to lease me the Meadow Creek ranch."

Madigan stared, hardly daring to believe his luck. It seemed as though Landers of his own volition had already decided not to lease the ranch. "You mean . . . ?"

"I mean Uncle Glenn executed the lease himself before I left Tennessee." Tony opened a bag and took from it a legal paper. He handed it to the lawyer, who saw at once that it was a lease made directly from owner to tenant.

After a moment of dismay Madigan brightened. This should take him off the hook with Max Charny. Charny's command was that he must *not* issue a lease to Tony Landers. Well, he wouldn't need to. The lease, issued by Hollister himself, had already been in existence before Charny's command.

"Uncle Glenn," Tony went on, "also gave me a letter of introduction to a friend of his, a stockman named Jerry DeSpain. Know him?"

"Of course. DeSpain runs cattle and sheep all over the county. He keeps an office in the DeSpain Block right here in town."

"Uncle Glenn said I'll need an experienced foreman and he wants Mr. DeSpain to steer me to one. My uncle said anyone recommended by Mr. DeSpain is sure to be on the level."

Madigan quickly agreed. "Your uncle and Jerry DeSpain, I remember, were close personal friends."

"Uncle Glenn," Tony explained, "figured I'll need about twenty thousand dollars to stock the place. So he arranged credit for me in that amount at a Portland bank. Before I left Tennessee I gave him my note for that sum. I'd be a cinch to get cheated," he admitted with a grin, "if I tried to buy cattle on my own judgment. That's why I have to take on a reliable foreman and let him do the buying for me."

"You won't go wrong," Madigan agreed, "with anyone vouched for by DeSpain. Good night, Tony. See you in the morning."

The streets were dark when Madigan left the hotel. He hurried to the Walla Walla Club. Helena, the fascinating hostess, waved a hand to him as he passed through the barroom. The man with her was Sol Olcutt, second in command here. Ignoring them, Madigan went on to Charny's private office at the rear.

The pressure of his news made him burst in without knocking. "Look, Max," he broke out, "just learned I don't have anything to say about the Hollister ranch lease. Glenn Hollister signed it himself in Tennessee before the nephew left there."

Charny have him a hard stare. "How do you know? Don't try to weasel out on me, Madigan."

"I just saw the lease. It's made direct from uncle to nephew. The boy got in on this evening's stage..."

"There was a girl with him," Charny cut in. "Who is she?"

"She's another of my clients; the Costain niece from Michigan. They just happened to be on the same stage. Landers has a letter of introduction to Jerry DeSpain. And a twenty-thousand-dollar credit in a Portland bank to buy livestock with. He..."

The gambler's eyes narrowed shrewdly. "Say that again, Madigan."

The lawyer said it again, in detail.

It brought a gleam to Max Charny's agate-black eyes. He pressed a buzzer which promptly summoned Sol Olcutt from the barroom. "This fella givin' you any trouble, boss?" Olcutt was a tall, lean man with iron-colored cheeks and a short moustache which matched the blackness of his hair. He fixed a speculative gaze on Madigan.

"Not at all," Charny assured him. "Fact is, things are lookin' up. Sit down, Sol, and listen to his tip-off. Sounds like a gold mine, if we work it right."

Again Madigan repeated what he'd learned from Tony Landers in Room 108.

"Our break," Charny told them, "is that Jerry

DeSpain went to The Dalles on a big sheep deal this morning. He'll be tied up there for a week. Now listen, Madigan, in the morning you round up young Landers and take him to Room Number One in the DeSpain Block. That's Jerry's private office; just a cubbyhole he uses to answer his mail and keep his accounts. In the morning you walk in there with Landers and introduce him to Jerry DeSpain."

Both Madigan and Olcutt gaped in confusion. The lawyer exclaimed, "But you just said DeSpain's out of town."

Charny smiled and turned to Olcutt. "Sol, get yourself a corduroy riding coat, a pair of spurs, and a tall, cowman's hat. And one of those skeleton keys you can buy for a nickel at any hardware store. Be sitting at DeSpain's desk at nine in the morning. When Madigan comes in with Landers he'll say, 'Hello, Jerry; meet Tony Landers from Tennessee. He's got a letter of introduction to you from Genn Hollister.' "

An alarmed protest came from Madigan. "You can't get away with it! It'd fool the boy for the time being but not for long. Someday he's sure to run into DeSpain and then . . ."

"Shut up!" Charny's voice whiplashed. "You'll do exactly as I say. Don't forget I've got Kent Durwin for a hole card. Cross me and I'll turn him loose on the courthouse lawn."

The threat froze Madigan. He could only stand

by, wretchedly helpless, as Charny finished his instructions to Olcutt.

"You shake hands with the boy, Sol, and inquire about his uncle's health. Then you read the letter of introduction. It asks you to recommend a reliable foreman who'll help Landers buy cattle to start ranching with. You know just the man. Tex Gresham."

"Tex Gresham!" Olcutt echoed. "You mean we rig up for Gresham to ramrod the kid's ranch? He advises the kid how and where to pick up twenty-thousand-dollars' worth of cows?"

"Why not?" Charny lowered an eyelid. "That twenty thousand dollars is a blue chip we hadn't counted on. Might as well rake it in. The other stake'll keep for a while. We can pick it up later."

Shocked speechless for a moment, Madigan finally found tongue. "Listen, Max, I don't want anything to do with this. Leave me out of it. I can just point out the DeSpain Block to Landers and tell him to go up to Room Number One on the second floor. That way I won't know anything about Olcutt pretending to be DeSpain."

Charny shook his head. "You'll go all the way into that office," he demanded, "and shake hands with Sol. You'll call him Jerry and present Landers. Then you can get the hell out of there and leave things to me and Sol. That's all for now. If I need you for anything else I'll whistle."

When Madigan left the office Olcutt broke into

laughter. "Tex Gresham! It's a smart pick, boss. Tex advisin' a sucker how to buy cows! Well, Tex oughta know a good cow when he sees one—he's stolen enough of 'em." Then Olcutt sobered as another thought struck him. "But look! What about the other jackpot on the Hollister ranch? The one Roy Hollister stashed there just before a hot trigger from Kansas came along and gunned him down."

"That stake'll still be there," Charny assured him, "after we pick Landers clean and get rid of him. With a lease on the ranch we'll have plenty of time to find it. We know it's within sight of Roy's bedroom window—according to the letter he wrote Helena telling her to join him in Oregon."

"That's right," Olcutt remembered. "But by the time she got here Roy was dead and buried. Does she know anything about this Tex Gresham setup?"

"Not a thing, Sol. Now start rigging yourself up to look like a big-time cowman. Then hunt up Gresham and tell him to stand by."

IX

A piny smell came through a high barred window and made Kent Durwin aware that he was somewhere deep in a forest. The room was barely wide enough for the cot he lay on and its door was bolted on the other side. For two days he'd known what was going on around him and his memory of the recent week had only a few blank spots. The men who'd brought him here called themselves Murph and Jody. He had to admit that they'd fed him well and had given him no unnecessary rough treatment.

Their manner was entirely impersonal and the only question they'd asked him was, "You beginnin' to remember things, buddy?"

At his nod they'd seemed pleased rather than otherwise. So the man paying them couldn't be Douglas Madigan. Madigan wouldn't want him to remember things. Madigan had lured him to a bridge and dropped him into a cold, fast river. That much Kent Durwin now remembered clearly.

Only vaguely he remembered the pretty brown-eyed face of a girl in a nurse's cap, bending over him, feeding him warm soup with a spoon. There'd been a long bumpy ride in a buckboard. They'd blindfolded him during the last hours of it. Not that he could have seen much, in the darkness. He knew that toward the end of the second night when he'd arrived here he'd heard wheels splashing across running water. He'd never seen the outside of this cabin or any part of the inside except this narrow space probably meant for the storage of food. One wall had shelves, and the small, high, barred window would have kept thieves out. Hunters, trappers, or lumbermen might have once used the place.

The door opened and Murph came in with a platter of food. Murph was the short one. Like Jody he wore a holstered .45. Both men had arrived here shaggy but were now clean-shaven. Each wore a belted corduroy coat and a hunter's corduroy cap.

"How long do you aim to keep me here?"

Kent didn't expect an answer and was surprised when Murph gave him one. "Just as long, buddy, as the lawyer fella does what the boss says."

"Okay. Suppose the lawyer doesn't obey the boss. What happens then?"

"In that case," Murph answered with a grin, "we turn you loose and let nature take its course."

When he was alone Kent lay for hours trying to assess that cryptic reply. If he were set free, what would he naturally do? He'd go straight to Pendleton and tell the sheriff just what had happened at midnight on a bridge. It was a sword, clearly, which Murph's employer was holding over Madigan's head.

• • •

Kent slept soundly that night and Murph brought him a bacon breakfast. It was a sunny day with a squirrel scolding on a pine limb outside the high, barred window. Then, in midmorning, Jody came hurriedly into the room. "Sorry, buddy, but looks like we're about to have a visitor. Means I've got to shut you up."

He used pigging strings to tie Ken's wrists and ankles, then wadded a rag and stuffed it into the prisoner's mouth. "I'll take it out," he promised, "soon as the fella moves on."

Murph opened the door and gave a hushed warning. "He's headin' right this way, Jody. I've seen him in town, more 'n once. Name's McDowd and he's a deputy sheriff."

Jody grimaced. "Good thing we got rid of that buckboard. We're up here for a little huntin' and fishin', remember."

"That's what I'll tell him," Murph said. "You stay in here with Durwin. If the fella gets too nosey, only one thing we can do."

"Only one thing," Jody agreed. He drew his .45, twirled the cylinder, checked the loads. Then he aimed it breast high at the door which Murph had just closed. Helpless on the cot, Kent Durwin could nevertheless hear everything. He heard a rider dismount in front and enter the cabin's main room with clinking spurs.

There was a bluff greeting from Murph. "Make

yourself at home, Sheriff. Sit and I'll pour you a cup of coffee."

"Thanks. I'm lookin' for two men in a wagon. Maybe a spring wagon. They shanghaied a sick man in Pendleton and took off with him. Seen anybody like that up this way?"

"Nope. Few days ago a family of Umatillas passed this way on ponies. Haven't seen anybody else for a week. What do these two birds look like?"

"One short, one tall, both shaggy with face hair. Black slouch hats. The fella they took off with is a good-lookin' young chap named Durwin. Sandy complexion. He was in bad shape and maybe they've finished him off by now . . . Thanks."

A silence while the visitor sipped coffee. Then, "You up here all by yourself?"

"Nope. Me and a pard of mine are out for a little huntin' and fishin'. Ben Hockaday from Walla Walla. Right now he's out tryin' to pick up a brace of grouse for supper."

Another silence, longer this time. Kent could imagine the deputy sizing up the room—and sizing up Murph. Was he looking at this bolted door?

A growing dread gripped Kent. If the lawman should insist on searching the cabin he'd most certainly be shot dead. Jody's .45 was cocked and aimed at the closed door. If the visitor should open that door he'd be between two fires—Jody in front and Murph behind him. After shooting the lawman they'd have no choice other than to give the same treatment to a witness—Kent Durwin.

Tension eased when the deputy changed the subject. "If you see a skinny guy on a buckskin ride by here, better throw down on him and fetch him to town. You could pick up a reward from Wells-Fargo."

"Yeh? What's he wanted for?"

"He and a toughie named Cass Clardy held up a stagecoach near Meacham. A deputy sheriff came along in time to blast Clardy out of his saddle but the other man got away."

"If we see the guy," Murph promised, "we'll hold him for you. 'Nother cup of coffee?"

"No thanks. Got to push on. Wanta make Meacham in time for supper."

Kent heard the deputy leave the cabin and ride away. Jody lowered his gun and holstered it, "That was a close one, buddy. If he'd come nosin' in here, only one thing I could do."

Tony Landers sat with his hat on his knees waiting for Sol Olcutt to finish reading Glenn Hollister's letter of introduction. Presently the man at the desk looked up with a smile. "I know just the man you need, my boy. Tex Gresham. Tex is a right smart horse- and cowman. He happens to be between jobs right now. I can send him around to you, if you like."

"Thanks, Mr. DeSpain. Want to get started for the ranch quick as I can. First I'll have to pick up an outfit."

"That's right. A buckboard and team with a load of supplies. Couple of saddle horses and maybe a pack mare. Tex can pick 'em out for you and see that you don't get cheated."

"My check's good at a Portland bank, Mr. DeSpain. Gresham can find me in Room 108 at the Villard House."

Not to take up too much of this important cattleman's time, Tony left the office.

Douglas Madigan had ushered him up there but had remained only long enough to make the introduction. Something oddly restrained in the lawyer's manner had puzzled Tony.

He was heading back to the Villard House when he met Donna Costain. She was in a gay mood this morning. "I'm out seeing the town," she announced. "Come be my escort, Tony."

Nothing could suit him better. Together they strolled down one side of Main and up the other. They passed four large general stores, three livery barns, two drugstores, the old Pendleton Hotel, a blacksmith shop, four restaurants, and a dozen saloons. Just opposite the courthouse a brick building had the name Hollister Block on its coping and Donna exclaimed brightly, "This must belong to your Uncle Glenn. From what I've heard, he must own half the town."

Shingles at the foot of the stairs indicated that several doctors had second-floor offices. "You should have that head cut redressed," Donna insisted. "They did the best they could for you at Pelican; but here's a chance to have it done right."

Overriding Tony's objection the girl made him go upstairs. There they found a reception room where a pretty, dark-haired nurse was presiding. Tony took off his hat and touched the taped cut on his scalp. "She says I ought to have it looked at."

"Doctor Egan isn't busy right now. Come along." Nancy Rollins led him down a corridor and presently returned to join Donna. "I'm Nancy Rollins. And you're Donna Costain, of course. Everyone in town is talking about the stage holdup at Meacham. You own the ranch on East Birch Creek, don't you?"

Donna liked her at once. "Yes. Have you ever been out there?"

"No. But a friend of mine went out there twice about a week ago. And he found out something." Nancy's face clouded. "Something which made someone try to kill him. Did you hear about it?"

"No. Tell me, please."

"First, let me show you a note he poked under this door at midnight." Nancy took it from a desk drawer and Donna saw a line of writing:

Miss Rollins: Your doctor was right and everyone else wrong. K.D.

By the time Tony's scalp cut had been retaped by Doctor Egan, Nancy had given Donna an account of the adventures and mishaps which had befallen Kent Durwin. "We can't imagine," she finished, "why anyone would want to steal him out of a hospital bed in the middle of the night. But it must have something to do with what he found out at your Birch Creek ranch."

"We were exploring the town," Tony said as he rejoined them. "We did Main Street, both sides. Anything else we oughta see?"

"You might take a look at your uncle's town house," Nancy suggested. "It's not far from here. If you like, I'll point it out."

She went down to the street with them and guided them two blocks west to the corner of Alta and Willow. There she pointed out an imposing two-story frame residence with a fenced front yard. "The LaDows live here now, as renters," Nancy said. "That's Judge LaDow's buggy tied in front."

Tony chuckled. "I'd know it was Uncle Glenn's house, even if you hadn't told me."

Nancy looked at him curiously. "How could you tell?"

"He's got a hitching post just like that one in front of his house in Tennessee."

The post was a three-inch pipe topped by a cast-iron horse's head. A ring in the horse's mouth had the snap of a hitching rein in it, the other end of the rein being attached to the bridle bit of the buggy horse which stood by it. A lady, dressed for shopping, now came out of the house and went to the buggy. She unsnapped the hitch rein, then used the stone carriage block to mount into the buggy. Gathering up the driving reins she drove off toward the shopping district of the town.

"What else would you like to see?" Nancy asked.

"We've seen everything but the river," Donna said, "and the bridge you were telling me about."

They went back to Main Street and turned north. The roar of the raging Umatilla River filled the air as they came to the bridge. At the middle of it they looked down on a turbulent torrent.

"Is this," Donna asked with a shiver, "where it happened?"

"Yes. At midnight just a few minutes after he slipped the note under my door."

They stood silently at the bridge rail, staring at the rough, icy water sweeping beneath them. Nancy Rollins, her mind fastened solemnly on Kent Durwin, spoke more to herself than to the others. "He came back alive out of that; so maybe he'll come back from wherever he is now."

"I'll bet he does," Tony said, as they walked

off the bridge. At the Villard House he left them, Nancy returning to her receptionist duties, Donna calling at Douglas Madigan's office to ask why he hadn't sold her ranch, and Tony to wait in his room for Tex Gresham.

X

As he passed through the hotel lobby Tony bought today's issue of the local newspaper, the *East Oregonian*. He went down the hall toward Room 108 and as he neared it two of his recent stagemates came out of 106. He waved a greeting. "Howdy, folks. How do you like Pendleton by this time?"

Mrs. Horace Mumford gave him a restrained smile. Her husband said, "Haven't seen much of it yet." The two moved on toward the lobby. They'd been like that on the stage; uncommunicative.

Tony went into 108, made himself comfortable, then began looking through his newspaper. There was an account of the attempted stage robbery near Meacham, giving the names of the coach passengers.

There were advertisements of the Pioneer Livery Stable, the Umatilla Sales Stables, the Folsom Blacksmith Shop, the Walla Walla Club, and a dozen or more saloons. John Hailey's stage line posted its schedule of arrivals and departures.

An editorial bemoaned the fact that law officers had so far failed to expose and capture what was clearly an organized gang of outlaws which for past months had been preying on ranchers, wagon trains, and stagecoaches through eastern Oregon. "Many of us suspect," the article concluded, "that operations of the gang are being directed from right here in Pendleton."

Further down the page the name Jerry DeSpain caught Tony's eye but before he could read more there was a knock. He laid the paper aside and opened the door. A tall, swarthy, capable-looking man stood there.

The man was smooth-shaven, black-haired under a range hat, broad at the shoulders and narrow at the hips. He wore leathers from throat to spurs. "I'm Gresham," he announced quietly. "Jerry DeSpain told me to look you up."

"We can talk here," Tony offered. "Or would you rather we'd go into the bar?"

"Right here suits me."

"My uncle told me to depend on Mr. DeSpain's judgment," Tony said. "So far as I'm concerned you're hired right now. What's top pay for a ranch foreman?"

"Sixty a month and found," Gresham said. "Saddle hands get just half that."

"Okay. How many saddle hands will we need?"

"Right at first—only you and me plus a cook. Main thing's a couple of saddle outfits and a buckboard loaded with grub. We could pick 'em up today and get started early tomorrow. Take us from sunup till dark to make Meadow Creek. I already wrote down a list of stuff we ought to have."

Tony looked at the list Gresham handed him.

Besides four horses and a buckboard, it called for two saddles, bridles, harness, lamp oil, blankets, and several hundred pounds of staple groceries.

"Top of that," Gresham suggested, "you'll need to outfit yourself: boots, denims, a few wool shirts. Nights get kinda cold down there."

"My check's good at a Portland bank," Tony said. "Suppose we divide up this list. I'll buy the grub, blankets, clothing, and stuff; you pick out everything else."

"Suits me, Mr. Landers."

"Call me Tony." Tony took two sheets of hotel stationery and on one made a list of things he must select himself, on the other a list to be picked up by Gresham. While he was doing it Gresham glanced through the local newspaper which Tony had laid aside. From it he tore a double column which advertised three stores: The Blue Front; Switzer's; Alexander & Frazier.

He handed the store ads to Tony. "You can get what you want at those three places. Have the stuff delivered to the Umatilla Sales Stables on south Cottonwood Street. That's where I'll get the buckboard and horses. I know a good Mexican cook I can hire."

Soon everything was settled. It meant a busy afternoon for both men, each independent of the other. "I'll load up tonight," Tex promised. "Then I'll drive up here at daybreak with our outfit, cook, saddle stock, and all."

• • •

Gresham left the hotel and hurried to the Walla Walla Club. Glancing over his shoulder to make sure his employer hadn't followed him, he turned in there. In a very few minutes he was tapping on the door of Max Charny's private office.

Charny and Olcutt were waiting for him. "Everything's set," he reported. "But we had one hell of a narrow squeak."

"What went wrong?" Charny demanded.

"Nothing. But it might have. He was reading today's paper when I went in there and if I'd been a minute later he could have seen this." From under his jacket Gresham took half of Page 3 which he'd managed to tear off and conceal while recommending the three stores to Tony Landers.

A local news item in the scrap he'd retained said:

> Jerry DeSpain has gone to The Dalles, where he'll spend several days negotiating a big sheep deal. Don't let them put anything over on you, Jerry.

Charny read the item. "We'd be scuttled," he admitted, "if the kid had seen that. Get him out of town quick as you can, Tex."

"And once you get him outa town," Olcutt

added, "you gotta make damned sure he never comes back."

"How long," Gresham queried, "is this operation gonna take?"

"It's got two angles," Charny reminded them. "First, we've got to con the boy out of his Portland bank money. Next, we've got to find the Kansas mail loot that Roy Hollister stashed somewhere near the ranch house. So that we'd have plenty of time to hunt for it, I wanted to lease the place. But now maybe we won't need any lease. Just kid the boy along for a while, Tex, and I'll send you orders by Frenchy."

Gresham went out and walked two blocks south to the Umatilla Sales Stables, where he began negotiating for four horses, saddles, harness, and a buckboard. The place was a reputable concern and Jess Cummings, who ran it, knew Gresham only as an experienced cattle hand. "If you'll check with Tony Landers at the Villard House," Tex suggested, "you'll find he's just hired me as foreman. He's Glenn Hollister's nephew and I'm helping him outfit the Meadow Creek ranch."

Hollister was a name to conjure with in this county. After sending a clerk to the Villard House for confirmation, Jess Cummings began dealing. This part of the operation had to be entirely on the level and Gresham made it so by haggling for the best bargains possible.

"Landers is uptown buying the grub and stuff,"

he said to Cummings. "He'll have it delivered here so I can load up and get a daybreak start."

"You mean I can go along and help you spend money?" Donna exclaimed as she took luncheon with Tony. "I just love to spend money so let's be at it right away."

It was late afternoon when they finished at Switzer Brothers, where Tony bought boots, shirts, and riding leathers for himself. This, Tony knew as they went back to the Villard House, would be his last evening with Donna for a long time. "Meet me for dinner in half an hour," he said as he parted from her in the lobby.

Dinner turned out to be a foursome for as they entered the dining room Nancy Rollins beckoned them. She was at a table with Douglas Madigan. "I've just spent bushels of Tony's money," Donna said happily as she joined them.

"Tex Gresham spent a lot more of it," Tony added. "We'll be pulling out for the ranch before you city folks are up in the morning."

A little later it occurred to Tony that he and the girls had done all the talking. Madigan seemed uneasily preoccupied. He kept looking around at other diners as though fearful of some embarrassing approach.

The only one who approached them was Jess Cummings, who came to the table and spoke to Tony. "Sorry to bother you, Mr. Landers. But your foreman says you'll be leaving at daybreak so maybe you'd like to take care of this tonight." He presented a statement of purchases made by Gresham.

The total was no more than Tony had expected. He went out to the lobby with Cummings and borrowed a desk pen. After writing a check he took a receipt and returned to his dinner companions. "Next buy I make," he told them, "will be for stock cattle. Wonder where Tex'll pick 'em up."

Nancy asked, "How did you get on to him, Tony?"

Before Tony could answer, Madigan cut in hurriedly. "He got on to him through me, Nancy." It was a frantic diversion to keep Jerry DeSpain's name from being mentioned.

There were other tight corners for Madigan before dinner was over. In the lobby he said a hurried good-bye. "I've a client meeting me at the office," he told Nancy. "So I'd better take you home right now."

There was nothing hurried about Tony's good-bye to Donna. They sat at a lobby window, watching the Court Street traffic flow by.

"How long will you be staying in Pendleton, Donna?"

"First," she said, "I have to sell my ranch. I'll take the first fair offer I get and then perhaps invest the money in a dress shop, or millinery store, here in Pendleton."

"More likely you'll marry a rancher and settle down."

When she didn't respond Tony added, "Which wouldn't be a bad idea provided you picked the right rancher."

"Do you have one in mind?"

"How did you guess? Wait till I make good on that Meadow Creek lease and I'll come loping into town to tell you who he is."

Presently he took her to the foot of the stairs, then on an impulse went all the way to the upper floor with her. Outside her room door she said, "Good-bye, Tony. You'll be gone before I get up in the morning."

"In that case why not say good-bye the right way?" She didn't protest when Tony took her cheeks between his hands and kissed her lips.

It still lacked half an hour of midnight when he went to bed in Room 108, on the ground floor. He lay quietly for a while, thinking pleasantly of Donna Costain. How often could he come to town to see her? It was a ten-hour ride each way. She'd have other attentions here. He couldn't risk staying away too long.

Just as he was falling asleep he heard a sound from the next room. When he heard it again it seemed to be a moan of someone in distress. A woman? The next room was Number 106 and the Horace Mumfords were in there.

When the moaning was again repeated, Tony

got up and put on a dressing gown. He went out into the hall and moved one door to the left. Distinct sounds came from beyond it. Distress sounds! Also footsteps moving about the room.

Tony tried the door and it wasn't locked. The Mumfords, before going to bed, would have locked it. But an intruder with a skeleton key could have unlocked it. Tony pushed the door open and saw a lamplighted room and a man with one leg out a window. The Mumfords lay in bed, Horace Mumford with a bleeding head and apparently dead or stunned. His wife lay beside him half paralyzed with terror.

The intruder about to escape through an open window was small, shabby, and unmasked. He had a bag in one hand and a gun in the other. Half in and half out the window he twisted around and fired point-blank at Tony.

The bullet smashed into the door jamb at Tony's elbow. Then the man dropped out into the darkness and was gone.

A night clerk and porter came running from the lobby. Doors opened and guests came out into the hall. In a few minutes a dozen people were crowding into the Mumfords' room.

The last to appear was Town Marshal Ben Gray from the street. The porter was sent scurrying for a doctor. The night clerk bathed Horace Mumford's face and it brought the man to life.

His wife, still moaning, sat up in bed and pointed to something on the floor.

A woman guest from Room 105 picked it up and they all saw what it was. It was the sateen underskirt which Mrs. Mumford had worn here on her long train and stage journey from the east. The lining and ruffles had been ripped and slashed in a dozen places.

"Twenty-two thousand dollars!" Mrs. Mumford mourned wretchedly.

"Money you stole?" Marshal Gray demanded sternly of Mumford.

"No. Money I earned. Honest money," Mumford insisted. When he explained, Tony felt sure he was telling the truth.

XI

Tony gave Tex Gresham the highlights of it as they rode south out of town early in the morning. The laden buckboard which followed them was driven by the Mexican cook Gresham had picked up yesterday.

"The way Mumford tells it," he explained to Gresham, "he came here from Sioux City, Iowa, where he'd been running a feed store and livery barn for the last ten years. He'd done well and saved up twenty-two thousand dollars, plus some stock he owned in the local bank. He wasn't an officer of the bank, had nothing to do with it except that he'd invested in a few shares of stock. The bank went bust and left a lot of depositors holding the bag. Some of them began filing suits against officers and stockholders to recover their lost deposits. Mumford figured it wasn't fair, since the failure wasn't his fault. To make sure they didn't attach his money, he put it in his wife's petticoat and lit out for Oregon."

"What I can't savvy," Gresham pondered, "is how the fella knew they had that money in a skirt."

"Sheriff Martin has an idea about that," Tony said. "He told us there's an organized gang of thieves around here and they've got spies and lookouts right in Pendleton. The Mumfords acted nervous and scared on the stage and at the hotel after they got there. Lots of people noticed it. Maybe they figured Mumford was an absconding cashier, which he wasn't. A wide-awake thief could hear talk like that and make a play for whatever the Mumfords had on them."

They went on past the shanty of an Indian farmer and beyond it they saw an Indian boy herding a small band of sheep. "Your uncle's place," Gresham said, "is a piece south of the reservation."

"How many cows will it run, Tex?"

"Six or seven hundred, I figure, provided we grass 'em on government land through the summer. We oughta save the home ranch for winter pasture. It's four fenced sections on Meadow Creek; best grass in the county except maybe down on Camas Prairie."

"Where's Camas Prairie?"

"Not far southeast of your place. A right pretty range." Gresham went on to describe Camas Prairie as a circular basin twelve miles in diameter surrounded by piny hills and watered by four clear streams.

"Any stock ranches?"

"A few. One of 'em we oughta go see right away. It's Frank Wagner's Flying A outfit on Big Camas Creek."

"Why should we see Frank Wagner?"

"Because he's changing from cattle to sheep. Aims to sell out his cow herd and slap the money into woolies."

"So you think," Tony suggested, "that maybe we can buy his cows at a bargain?"

"It's worth a try. Wagner runs good stuff: whiteface natives."

At the head of Little McKay Creek they rested the horses for an hour. Pedro made a fire and put a coffeepot on it. Tony said, "I've heard Uncle Glenn mention a place called Paradise Prairie. Where is it?"

"We're on it now," Gresham told him. "It's a name some of the early settlers had for all this country south of the Umatilla River and west of the Blue Mountains."

As they moved on Pedro asked, "How many I cook for?"

"Just you and me and the boss," Tex said, "till we buy some cows."

During the afternoon ride Tex Gresham explained the fundamentals of western stock ranching. "In a nutshell," he finished, "summer your stuff on the open range and winter it at home. Put up enough hay to feed your horses when they're working. Make 'em live on grass when they're not. Feed a cow only in deep snow or when she's too thin at calving time."

They crossed East Birch Creek near its head and a tree there had a printed notice on it. A homesteader near the village of Albee was holding an auction sale three days from now. Chattel to be auctioned off was listed and Gresham made a note of certain items: a haymower and a sulky rake; a farm wagon with hayrick; a guernsey milch cow; miscellaneous barn tools.

"It'll pay us to ride over there and bid on that stuff," Tex advised. "We might get it pretty cheap."

They struck the mouth of Pearson Creek and rode up it in cool shade, holding a course almost due south. "We're off the Indian land now," Tex said.

Looking ahead Tony saw piny hills sloping up from lush grassy valleys. A dozen times he saw a bounding deer and at every creek crossing he glimpsed darting trout.

Just after sunset they topped a divide between Pearson Creek and Meadow Creek. It was mellow twilight when they hit Meadow Creek and followed easterly down it. "Looks like they've had plenty of rain along here," Tex observed. "Means we can get a right good crop of hay."

Two miles further on the creek valley widened and Tony saw buildings ahead. They were white buildings against the green of a cottonwood grove. They came to a gate in a wire fence. Beyond the gate they crossed an irrigation ditch running brim full. It circled the high edge of a bluestem meadow.

A second gate let them into a ranch yard where the main residence looked to Tony more like the house of a southern plantation than a western ranch dwelling. It was tall, wide, and white, with porch pillars, and with small dormer windows under the eaves marking an attic above the second floor. "Uncle Glenn never did believe in crowding himself," Tony said with a grin.

There was a hay barn, a bunkhouse, a storehouse, and a long shelter on the north side of a corral. The pulley well had two oaken buckets. No life was in sight. Nothing seemed to have been disturbed since the Pete Carter family had moved out a few days ago.

Glenn Hollister, on suddenly deciding to return to Tennessee three years ago, had taken nothing with him except personal family belongings. The place had been leased fully furnished to the Carters, even including dishes and kitchenware. "All you'll need to start housekeeping," he'd told Tony, "is blankets and grub."

He'd given Tony a door key and Tony let himself into a wide hallway from which carpeted stairs led upward. A parlor on one side and a dining room on the other had tables, chairs, oil lamps, and rugs. Mrs. Carter and her daughters had been proud housekeepers—not the kind who'd leave a house unswept for the next occupant.

Pedro unloaded his buckboard while Gresham

filled oil lamps and lighted them. While Pedro made supper they fed and watered the horses. Upstairs in the main house each man picked his bedroom and put blankets on a mattress.

Ten hours in the saddle had wearied Tony. He knew now that riding to Pendleton for a call on Donna would take a tough, physical effort plus three days of time—one to go, one to stay, one to return.

"What's on for tomorrow, Tex?"

Today was Friday. "We can spend Saturday and Sunday getting acquainted with the layout," Tex suggested. "Monday we oughta ride to Albee and maybe pick up a few bargains at that auction sale. Tuesday we can ride to Camas Prairie and see what Frank Wagner wants for his cows."

Max Charny was in Madigan's Hollister Block office. "That Landers boy'll be buyin' stock and equipment, Doug. A few ranch tools at first. Later he'll buy himself a herd of cattle."

"Yes? What of it?" Madigan stared glumly at his visitor. The gambler had walked in on him without an appointment.

"Every time he buys something he'll offer a check. The sellers'll wonder if the check's any good. So he'll mention your name as a reference. Everybody on this range knows you've been Glenn's agent for years. So they'll be askin' you if the boy's checks are okay."

"You mean they'll write me?"

"Maybe; or they may come clear to Pendleton to ask you in person. You say yes. You tell 'em Glenn leased his ranch to his nephew and staked him to a twenty-thousand-dollar account in a Portland bank. All of which is true."

But Madigan sensed that there was more to it. "If you're figuring to gyp him out of that bank account, Charny, I'll have nothing to do with it. I'll not..."

"Don't tell me what you won't do," Charny cut in. "You haven't forgotten, have you, that I'm still holding Kent Durwin? Want me to turn him loose?"

Again the threat brought a chill to Madigan. Durwin was a sword over his head.

"Young Landers," Charny reminded him, "has already written a few checks to Pendleton merchants. They'll be honored at the Portland bank. He'll write a few more small checks down on Meadow Creek, and they won't bounce. The bank'll get used to cashing them. Folks down around Camas Prairie'll get used to accepting them. It'll grease the wheels when the last check hits the bank—the big one given for a herd of cows."

But there won't be any cows! Madigan guessed shrewdly. Vaguely he began to see how they could work it. A series of small buys would be made in good faith, at fair prices, and the chattel properly delivered to the Meadow Creek ranch. A number of cattle herds would be inspected and bargained for without result. If the seller wanted $19,000.00, Gresham would offer a few thousand less and the deal would fall through.

"And when you're ready for the kill," Madigan prophesied, "Gresham will rush to his employer saying Rancher So-and-So is selling out under pressure. For spot cash he offers twenty-three-thousand-dollars' worth of cows for say seventeen thousand five hundred. So Landers makes out a check for seventeen five and signs it. Then Tex knocks him on the head and sends a fake So-and-So to Portland to cash the check. On the back of it will be written in Tony's handwriting, 'In full payment for so many head of cattle branded so-and-so.' It's what the bank's been expecting all along, so why should they refuse payment?"

Charny neither affirmed or denied it. "All of which is no skin off your neck, Madigan, as long as you know nothing about it. All you do is tell the truth. You answer any inquiry about the boy's credit by saying, 'Yes, his checks are good up to twenty thousand.'"

He didn't need to mention the alternative. Any defiance from Madigan would be a signal for Kent Durwin's release—perhaps right across the street on the courthouse lawn.

XII

At the Albee auction sale Tony let Gresham do the bidding. Today Gresham wore a cartridge belt with a holstered .45. "Lots of good folks down this way," he explained to Tony. "But there's a few bad actors and you've got to be ready for 'em."

When the sale was over the auctioneer totaled up the chattel bid in by Tex Gresham. One team of mules with harness; one hay wagon; one mower with extra blades; one sulky rake; two irrigation shovels; and one guernsey cow. "Comes to five hundred and forty-seven dollars, Mr. Landers."

As Tony began writing the check Gresham said quietly, "He's Glenn Hollister's nephew with a lease on the Meadow Creek ranch. The lease is in his pocket if you want to see it. Doug Madigan of Pendleton'll vouch for him."

Tony wrote on the back of the check, "In full payment for . . ." he listed the items purchased. His canceled check would serve as both title and receipt.

It was too late to start on the fourteen-mile trip back to Meadow Creek. They found cots in a loft over the Albee store-saloon and spent the night there. In the morning Tex hitched the span of mules to the wagon. Behind the wagon he hitched in tandem the sulky rake and the mower. The guernsey cow was used to a lead rope. Nevertheless Gresham was dubious as he tied the halter rope to the wagon's sideboard.

"Let's see how she goes." He climbed to the wagon seat and drove slowly a hundred yards. The mower and the rake rattled noisily behind him and the cow, after a few rebellious jerks, allowed herself to be led.

"I can make it, Tony, but it'll take eight or ten hours. You better ride on ahead."

Leading Gresham's saddled horse, Tony rode on ahead. It made him appreciate the man more than ever—taking on a tedious chore while he, Tony, would get home in time for a hot, noon meal.

There'd be one bad spot, Tex knew, at the crossing of Bear Wallow Creek. He'd probably need to take his three vehicles across separately. The crossing would be about two thirds of the way to the ranch. The cow pulled on her lead rope and many times Tex had to stop and rest her. The nine miles to Bear Wallow took him seven hours.

Gresham had to unhook his trailers, take the wagon across first, unhook the mules, and return twice for the mower and rake. By then it was midafternoon and Tony should be at the ranch taking it easy.

With all the trailers and the cow safely across Bear Wallow, Gresham put them in tandem again. Before he could climb to the wagon seat he saw a lone rider coming upcreek from the southeast. Camas Prairie lay that way, so Gresham waited for him while he licked the flap of a cigarette. A rider from Camas Prairie might know whether or not Frank Wagner had sold his Flying A cattle.

The oncomer looked and rode like a stock hand. His mount was a big sorrel and the stock of a carbine slanted upward from his saddle scabbard. As the rider came nearer his sun-browned face had a slightly familiar look. He wore a belt gun and the sun glinted on something shiny pinned to his jacket.

At once Gresham was alert. Sight of a law officer always alerted him. The law wasn't looking for him in Oregon; he could come and go as he pleased in Umatilla and adjacent counties. But it wasn't a star that fellow was wearing. The shiny thing wasn't shaped like a sheriff's badge. It was shield shaped—which could mean that he was a Deputy U.S. Marshal.

A minute more and Gresham was sure of it. Still standing behind his wagon, screened by it from the shoulders down, he loosened the flap of his gun holster. The sun-browned face seemed more and more familiar. The man reined to a stop about ten yards beyond the wagon.

"Howdy," the rider said. "Seen a couple of

horse traders go by here the last few hours?"

Gresham shook his head. "Just got here myself. What are they wanted for? Stealin' stock?"

"Not that. We want them for selling whiskey to Indians."

That was a federal offense. The shield on this rider's jacket said that he was a deputy marshal.

Tex lighted a cigarette. He could see all of the lawman and the lawman could see only the top fifteen inches of Gresham. "How far have you been trailin' 'em?" Tex asked.

"All the way from Boise City. They crossed the Snake yesterday and headed this way."

The man rode a little nearer and Gresham didn't like the way he was staring. Nor his sudden question—"You ever been up on the Big Wind in Wyoming?"

Tex tried to make his denial casual. "Nope. Nevada was my range till I came here."

"Your name wouldn't be Garfield, would it?"

Gresham knew he faced a showdown. A six-gun showdown right here on the bank of Bear Wallow. His name *was* Garfield and once he'd killed a postmaster on the Big Wind in Wyoming.

The officer was still staring. "You *look* like Garfield; and you talk like Garfield. Haven't seen him for two years, so I could be mistaken. You got anyone close by who'll identify you?"

"Sure I have. My boss on Meadow Creek. I'm foreman there and I'm heading home right now."

"Reckon I'll ride along with you," the marshal decided. "If your boss says you're okay I'll take his word for it."

Gresham didn't dare let it be decided that way. Any inquiry at all would arouse doubt, and maybe suspicion, in the mind of Tony Landers.

Gresham went to the rear of the wagon and stooped there, pretending to inspect the hitch between wagon and mower.

When he came erect again his gun was out and spouting lead. Even at that the lawman matched his first shot and the bullet burned Gresham. He felt a sting at his cheek as he fired again. The lawman's second shot was wild and the man slumped over his saddle horn. Gresham took no chances and kept shooting.

Then he leaned against a wagon wheel and wiped blood from his cheek. He'd need to tell Tony Landers that a brushy limb had swiped him.

Gresham went to the lawman and made sure he was dead. Getting him out of sight should be easy enough. Bear Wallow was lined with willows and wild fruit thickets; otherwise the near prairie horizons showed nothing but grass.

A card in the dead man's pocket gave his name as Whitcomb. Gresham draped the body over the saddle. From the wagon he took an irrigation shovel bought at the auction. Then he led the big sorrel down the creek bank a hundred yards or more, stopping at a sandy spot by a clump of willows.

In less than half an hour the dead man was buried under two feet of sand. Gresham took saddle, bridle, and saddle pad from the horse and hid them in the willows. The man's six-gun and carbine he stuffed down a badger hole. The sorrel itself he turned loose, slapping a flank to start it running. In time the animal would be found grazing free, probably with a band of range mares. The assumption would be that its owner had caught up with the whiskey-selling traders he'd been trailing. No one would doubt that the men had resisted arrest and had come off on the long end of a gunfight.

Back at the wagon Tex Gresham threw all empty shells into the same riffles. With all signs of the encounter smoothed away he drove on toward the Meadow Creek ranch.

It was past sundown when his rattling tandem flanked by a trail-weary cow, stopped at the Hollister barn. He found Tony Landers there with a chunky, curly-haired man with a round, Latin face. "He's looking for a saddle job, Tex," Tony said.

"I am Jean Blanchette," the man said. "Any chance of getting on here?"

Gresham's blank stare gave no hint that he'd ever seen the man before. "Who've you been ridin' for, fella?"

"The Stirrup outfit down around Glenn's Ferry, Idaho. Ever hear of it?"

The foreman nodded. "A good outfit. You got your own pony and saddle gear?"

"Yes; all I need's a bunk to spread my blanket roll on."

Tex turned to Tony. "We could put him to work irrigating while we're out looking at cattle."

"Anything you say, Tex."

"All right, Blanchette. Start out by unharnessing these mules. Stake the cow out in the best grass you can find; then join us at supper."

"Any trouble on the way?" Tony asked as he walked with his foreman to the main house.

"None at all, Tony."

After dark the new hand joined them and Pedro served them ham and hot cornbread. "We'll call you John," Gresham told the man. "You're not too proud to use a spade and pitchfork, I hope."

"I'd just as soon put up hay as brand calves," the man said.

He went back to the bunkhouse with kerosene for the lamp there. Later Gresham said, "I'll go see if he's got enough blankets, Tony."

When he got to the bunkhouse the new hand met him with a wink. "He hasn't smelled anything yet, has he, Tex?"

"Not a whiff, Frenchy. Did Sol send along any orders?"

"The deal stands just like he told you before,

Tex. You make a few small buys and haggle on a few big ones before turning them down. Every chance you get you refer people to Doug Madigan at Pendleton. You polish up that credit at the Portland bank with a string of chicken feed checks—and be sure he writes on the back just what they're spent for. Keep everything honor bright till time comes to write the last check, the big one, the payoff check. Then we . . ."

"I know what to do after that," Gresham broke in. "What about the other stake? The one Roy Hollister stashed here."

"I'm to spend my time looking for it whenever you ride off with the boss. Have you found out which was Roy's bedroom?"

"He slept in a back room upstairs. No use looking anywhere that can't be seen from its window."

"The barn, corrals, and sheds are on that side," Frenchy said, "Reckon he buried it, somewhere?"

"Maybe; and maybe not. All the letter to Helena said was that it's a spot he could see from his room window. But don't do any digging, Frenchy." A hard glint came to Gresham's eyes. "If you find it, better not try a run-out. Sol doesn't like double-crossers; neither does Max Charny."

"All I want is my cut, Tex."

"What about the Pendleton lawyer? Is he standing hitched?"

"Just like a buggy horse." Frenchy took a pint of whiskey from his blanket roll and stood treat with it.

"Breakfast at six, John," Gresham said with a grin. "Good night."

XIII

Douglas Madigan unlocked his Hollister Block office at nine in the morning. He raised a window to brighten the room, then settled at his desk. A copy of the *East Oregonian* lay on it and he knew he hadn't left it there himself.

Had one of yesterday's clients dropped it? It was a three-day-old paper. The date on it was June 19th and this was the 22nd.

Madigan's eyes blinked when he saw a name written in large letters across page one. It was a signature in ink and the name was *KENT DURWIN*.

In a minute the meaning of it hit Madigan hard. Durwin had been abducted on June 15th. This signature proved that he'd been alive four days later.

Max Charny, or some agent of Charny's, must have slipped in during the night to lay the newspaper on this desk. Why? Charny's whip over Madigan was a living hostage. Unless Durwin was alive, the threat could have no bite. "How do I know," Madigan had protested to Charny, "that you haven't already slit his throat?"

Well, this signed newspaper was a way of letting him know. At least until the 19th Kent Durwin had been kept alive. Madigan felt sure the signature was Durwin's. He could check the handwriting by comparing it with Durwin's registration at the Villard House.

A knock at his door made him put the newspaper out of sight. The caller who came in was Donna Costain.

She smiled as he held a chair for her. "I hope you won't think I'm impatient, Mr. Madigan. But I can't understand . . ."

"I know," he broke in. "You can't understand why your Birch Creek property is still unsold. Several times I've been offered ten thousand for it; but I've been holding out for twelve."

"Which perhaps is too much," the girl suggested.

"I'm sure it's not, because recently a prospect offered me twelve thousand. But he wanted me to take part payment and his note for the balance. He was a stranger in town so I turned him down."

"Who was he?" Donna asked.

"He's the Denver man who disappeared from Doctor McKay's clinic. You heard what happened to him, perhaps?"

"Yes. People have been talking about it. When did you last see him, Mr. Madigan?"

"Let's see." Madigan appeared to be thinking back. "He came directly to my office and said he wanted to see the place. I loaned him a key to the house. Early next morning he rented a horse and rode out there. Got back late in the afternoon;

called here to say he liked the place and would buy it at my price if I'd accept his note for part payment. Maybe I shouldn't have turned him down, but I did. I never saw him again."

As Donna left the office he listened to hear her footsteps descending the stairs. When he didn't, he guessed that she'd crossed the hall to Nancy's reception room.

He was certain of it a few minutes later when he left to attend court. The reception-room door was open and he saw the two girls talking intimately together. It was sure to be about Kent Durwin. They had a common interest in him; Nancy perhaps a romantic interest and Donna, who'd never met him, now knew that he was the one person who'd offered to buy her property at the asking price.

Madigan crossed to the courthouse. It took only a few minutes to file a petition before Judge LaDow. On the way out he stopped at the sheriff's office to ask if anything had been learned about Durwin. "It's got us buffaloed," Deputy Sargent told him. "Chances are those fellas have finished him off by now and chucked him into the river."

Madigan knew that they hadn't. At least they'd kept Durwin alive for the first four days.

At eleven o'clock Madigan went back to his office. His first thought was of the signed newspaper dated the 19th of June. At noon he must compare the writing with the hotel registration.

Madigan lifted the blotter . . . then stared at the bare oak of the desk top. The newspaper wasn't there! During the last hour someone had slipped in to take it away. A locked door would hardly be a problem. If Sol Olcutt could get a skeleton key to fit Jerry DeSpain's office, he could just as easily get a key to this one.

Why would Olcutt, or Charny, or some pussyfooting agent of theirs, leave a newspaper on this desk and then come back to take it away? A moment's thought gave Madigan the answer. They wanted him to see it, and be convinced that Durwin was alive, but they didn't want anyone else to see it. Once it had served their purpose they'd taken it away.

As he reached that conclusion the office door opened and a farmerish-looking man with red whiskers came in. Madigan had never seen him before.

"I'm Job Adamson of Ukiah," the man said. The card he presented identified him as a public auctioneer. "Just took in this check down at Albee." He exposed a check for five hundred and forty-seven dollars signed by Tony Landers. "Hope it don't bounce on me. The fella gave you as a reference."

Madigan looked at the check and nodded. A memory of Charny's threat made him add, "He's got credit at that bank up to twenty thousand dollars to buy stock and equipment with. He's Glenn Hollister's nephew and he's taking over the Meadow Creek ranch."

The auctioneer grinned, relieved. "That's all I want to know."

After Adamson left, Madigan sat staring dejectedly into space. There'd be other calls like this one. Always he'd have to say yes. Whether he liked it or not, he was helping Max Charny set Tony up for the kill.

At twelve o'clock the two girls across the hall went down to take lunch together.

They went into the Delmonico. A raw-boned Swedish waitress there was a favorite of Nancy's. "We only have time for sandwiches and coffee, Helga," Nancy said.

When the sandwiches came Helga asked, "Shall I bring some catsup? Some use it and some don't."

"Not for me, Helga. What about you, Donna?"

"I've a weakness for it, please," Donna admitted.

The waitress brought the catsup. "Now don't make off with it, ladies, like those two men did one night last week."

She said it lightly; but the term *two men* made Nancy alert. "What night last week, Helga?"

The waitress had to think a minute. "I remember; next morning I took a day off and went to Umatilla Landing. That was the sixteenth.

So it was late the evening of the fifteenth when those two men were in here. What they wanted that catsup bottle for I don't know. It was less than half full . . ."

"Do you know who they were?"

"Sure I do. They'd been in here before. One of them was Con Murphy; he called the other man Jody . . ."

"Don't say anything about this," Nancy warned. "It might be important."

When the Swedish girl left them Nancy spoke to Donna in an undertone. "Mrs. Olsen described those two men who came in at midnight. A tall man supporting a short man and she said he had blood on his shirt. When she told Doctor McKay about it he said, 'Blood from a catsup bottle, I'll wager.' It was the night of the fifteenth . . ."

"So what are we waiting for?" Donna exclaimed. "Let's go tell the sheriff."

They left the restaurant and crossed to the courthouse. Sheriff Martin wasn't in his office but Deputy Sargent was. They told him about two men named Murphy and Jody who'd made off with the catsup from the Delmonico.

"Jody's tall," Sargent remembered, "and Con Murphy's short. Wait a minute while I check with Ben Gray."

He went out looking for Town Marshal Ben Gray and presently came back with a report. "Those two no-gooders used to hang out at the

Maverick Bar. It's a rowdy joint and Gray makes a point of lookin' in there twice a day. He says till about the middle of the month Murph and Jody were there nearly every time he looked in. But since the middle of the month he hasn't seen 'em."

"So they must be the ones," Nancy concluded, "who fooled Mrs. Olsen and made off with Kent Durwin!"

"I'd bet on it," the deputy agreed. "That Maverick Saloon is a hangout for thugs. Like that fella Andy McDowd gunned down when he held up your stage, Miss Costain. Cass Clardy. Cass used to tend bar there and Murph and Jody make two more just like him."

Excitement flushed Donna's cheeks. "So what do we do?" she asked breathlessly.

"It's up to Sheriff Martin, Miss. My guess is he'll get a search warrant and organize a raid on the Maverick joint. It's long overdue, anyway. We can shake down everybody there and maybe make somebody snitch on Murph and Jody."

When Sheriff Martin came in the girls had gone. He listened to Sargent's report and made a quick decision. "We'll not only shake down everybody there, Bob, but we'll open the safe and see if it's got any secrets. Something smells about that place—something besides blood and gunpowder. Run up to Judge LaDow's office and get a search warrant."

• • •

The eight-man raiding crew were ready for action by late afternoon. The sheriff divided them into two teams of four. "Your crew'll go in from the alley, Bob, and mine'll go in from the street. At five o'clock on the dot. If anyone pulls a gun on us, blast him down."

At exactly five o'clock he pushed through the swinging half-doors with a level gun in his hand. Three of his men came in after him. At the same moment Bob Sargent and three raiders came in from the alley. Eight guns commanded the barroom and its fourteen inmates. Bartender Chips Kelly, ten male customers, and three short-skirted women stood frozen as the sheriff commanded, "We've got a court order; line up against the wall, everybody."

Only one man tried to get out. He was a newcomer in town who wore a checkered suit and a brown derby hat. This man made a dive for a side window. He was half out of it when Deputy McDowd winged him with a bullet.

"Acted like he's got something on his conscience, Andy," Martin said.

McDowd stooped for a close look. "His face," he reported, "sort of reminds me of a poster on Lot Livermore's post office wall. Wanted for a California killing, it says."

"Couple of you better go see who's upstairs," the sheriff directed.

Two of the raiders went up the steps and presently came down with three women and two men. They were lined up with the others.

"Frisk 'em," Martin ordered. "Bob, you begin at one end of the line, and John, you begin at the other. Anybody with a gun or knife on him goes to jail."

The search was made and six customers were found to be armed. The man shot through the leg had both a knife and a gun.

"Call a hack, Andy, and haul him to Doc McKay's clinic. Sperry, pick yourself a crew and help the other five bully-boys to the county jail. Everybody else stands by while we shake this dive down." Every drawer was pulled out; every box or bag or hamper was turned upside down. Nothing was overlooked. There were loaded dice and marked decks. A jar of knockout drops on the backbar gave a hint as to what had happened to Ed Pitcher and others who claimed to have been rolled here.

But there was nothing to connect with Con Murphy and Jody; or to the kidnapping of Kent Durwin.

"We've looked everywhere except in the safe," the sheriff said finally. "Kelly, open up the safe."

Chips Kelly, manager and day bartender, claimed he didn't have the combination.

"If you don't, who does?" Martin demanded.

"Don't know," Kelly said. "I only work here."

The sheriff turned to one of his men. "Okay, Dave, fetch a couple of sticks of dynamite. We'll blast the safe open."

As Dave started out, Chips Kelly spread his hands and gave up, "Aw right; I'll open it."

He kneeled before the safe, twisted knobs till the door came open.

One by one Sheriff Martin took various things from it and set them on the floor. There was cash which presumably had been taken in over the bar. Nothing incriminating seemed to be in the safe until the sheriff took out a bulky manila envelope, sealed, and with a name written on it. The name was Ranse Lanagan. Evidently Ranse Lanagan had put some valuables here either for concealment or safekeeping.

"He's a small-time hoodlum," Martin muttered. "Let's see what's in it." He opened the envelope and found money. The surprising amount of it made his eyes widen. There were 220 banknotes, each of a one-hundred-dollar denomination.

"Totes up to twenty-two thousand!" he announced after a count.

"Which is exactly," Bob Sargent remembered, "what somebody snitched out of the Mumford lady's underskirt!"

"Dave, scout every bar in town and see if you can pick up Ranse Lanagan."

"Anything else in the safe, Sheriff?"

"Nothing but this old newspaper." Martin took

a used newspaper from the safe, noting that it was a copy of the *East Oregonian* dated June 19th.

He was about to toss it aside when he saw writing across page one. A name had been signed there. The name *Kent Durwin!*

Deputies bunched around Martin to gape at the signature. They all knew that Durwin had been hauled away on the 15th.

XIV

Tony Landers sat between Tex Gresham and Frank Wagner on the top rail of a corral fence while Wagner's ranch crew drove Flying A cattle past them.

"My tally book," Wagner told them, "shows six hundred and twenty-eight head. Most of it's she-stuff two to five years old. You can have 'em at thirty dollars a round and I'll throw in the unweaned calves."

To Tony it seemed a fair price. The cattle were grade natives, Hereford stock; no longhorns among them. "What do you think, Tex?"

The lean, black-haired foreman did a little figuring on a scratch sheet. He gave the matter concentrated thought. Finally he shook his head. "I reckon you'll have to count us out, Mr. Wagner. Best offer we can make is twenty-seven dollars."

"I could get thirty-five," the Flying A man argued, "at the Omaha stockyards."

"Maybe," Tex admitted. "But you're a helluva long way from Omaha. You'd have to drive your stuff four hundred miles to the U.P. at Winnemucca, Nevada. That's your closest shipping point. Then you'd have to chounce 'em bawling into stock cars and pay freight on 'em to Omaha. After that you'd have to pay twelve dollars per car to whatever livestock commission company sells 'em for you. They'd be sold by the pound, not by the head; and they'll weigh a heap less in Omaha than they do right now. A four-hundred-mile trail drive plus a nine-hundred-mile train ride shrinks lot of tallow off of cows."

It was a true statement of fact and no one knew it better than Frank Wagner. But he was stubborn. "Thirty bucks a head is my price, boys. Take it or leave it."

Tony got down from the fence and shook hands with him. "Thanks for showing them to us, Mr. Wagner. If you happen to change your mind, please let us know."

The fifteen rough miles to Meadow Creek took three hours. In dim dusk they pulled up at the barn where Frenchy Blanchette was waiting for them. "Has Pedro got supper ready?"

"Ready and waitin'," Frenchy said. "Me, I've already et."

During the busy week which followed, Tony and his foreman made three other trips to bid on cattle. Whatever the price asked, in each case Gresham judged it to be too high. In each case his own bid was so low that the seller was sure to turn it down.

More and more it convinced Tony that his foreman was cannily guarding an employer's interests. "You can get poor paying too much for cows," Tex kept telling him, "and you can get rich paying too little. We keep on saying no till we get a rock bottom bargain."

Many times on these trips they picked up minor items of chattel. Haying tools; lariats; rock salt; a pair of weaning lambs for fall meat. Always Tony paid with a check, noting the item purchased on the check's back.

After Tony retired for the night, Gresham sometimes paid a quiet call on Frenchy at the bunkhouse. "How long we gotta keep this up, Tex?"

"We play it by ear from now on, Frenchy. The break'll come, maybe, when we bid on the Q Bar stuff down on the Little Day. Olcutt's got an angle on the Q Bar and he's sendin' Joe Forgy down here to line me out on it."

"Forgy throws a mean gun," Frenchy said.

"Just the same he used to be a cowhand and he looks the part. He'll show up lookin' for a job, just like you did. I'll advise Tony to take him on. I'll say we can use him at haying time. Meanwhile things are going okay. A string of checks are going through the Portland bank, all on the level; Tony's signature's on 'em and the stuff bought's all listed on the back; which oughta make our big check, when it shows up at the bank, plenty convincing."

"Then we got nothin' to worry about," Frenchy concluded.

"That's where you're wrong," Gresham corrected. "Suppose Tony wants to ride into Pendleton. Might happen any day. He's soft on a girl there and he's overdue for a date. A ten-hour ride each way. If he goes up one day he'd be too saddle-weary to ride back the next. So he'd lay over in town for the day in between."

"So what?"

"So he might run into Jerry DeSpain. Or he might drop in at the Walla Walla Club and see Sol Olcutt at the bar there."

Frenchy made a wry face.

"So we dassent let Tony go to town. If he tries it we've got to stop him. One way to stop him'd be to take a shoe off his horse. You can't ride far on a horse with three shoes on and one off."

"The horse'd go lame on him," Frenchy agreed, "before he'd gone a mile."

That was the third day of the month and a break came on the fourth. Tony Landers and his foreman had just finished the midday meal when they saw a rider coming from the southeast. He had the look of a cowboy and he was approaching from the wrong direction to be Joe Forgy.

As he dismounted at the house they saw that he was Eph Irons, foreman for Frank Wagner at the Flying A.

"Howdy, neighbors." Irons joined them on the

house porch. "You boys picked up a herd of cows yet?"

"Not yet," Gresham told him. "About time you're hitting the trail for Winnemucca, ain't it, Eph?"

Eph nodded. "Our drive starts bright and early in the morning."

"That's right," Tony Landers remembered. "Your boss said if he hadn't sold his cattle by the fifth, he'd start trailing them to the railroad."

"Which he'd just as soon not do," Eph Irons admitted, "if he can help it. So he wants to give you boys another crack at them."

Gresham cocked an eye. "You mean he's taking our bid? Twenty-seven dollars a head? He was holding out for thirty, last time I saw him."

"He offers to split the difference," the Flying A man announced. "Twenty-eight fifty. Whatta you say, boys?" He handed over a note from Frank Wagner confirming the offer.

Tony read it, then passed it to Gresham. "It's up to you, Tex."

For a moment Gresham seemed undecided. Then his jaw took a stubborn set and he shook his head. "Those cows aren't worth any more now than they were when I first looked at 'em. Our offer stands. Twenty-seven dollars. Not a dime more."

Irons shrugged and made no attempt to argue. "It's your money, boys, and our cows.

Winnemucca, here we come! What about a cup of coffee before I start back?"

They took him inside, where Pedro fed him. Frenchy grained the man's horse and let it rest unsaddled for an hour. By midafternoon Eph Irons was on his way back to the Flying A.

Frenchy had gone out to the hay meadow to spade water into the laterals. Gresham took a walk and joined him there. "Looks like we've hit pay dirt," he confided.

"Yeh? What's the deal?"

"Tonight I'm taking a ride," Tex explained. "It'll leave you alone with Landers. Whatever happens, make sure he doesn't leave the ranch. Soon as you get back to the corral, take a shoe off his horse."

"What if he decides to drive off in the buckboard?"

"Hide one of the neck yokes so he can't hitch up a team. Do anything you want, long as you keep him here on the ranch."

"Suppose the kid puts up a fight!"

"Pull a gun on him, if you have to. Be sweet as pie to him, though, at supper tonight. After tonight you can handle him rough. If he tries to get away, bat him down and then lock him up."

"Lock him up where, Tex?"

Gresham gazed off toward the tall, plantation-type ranch house built by Glenn Hollister. From under the high, gabled roof two small dormer windows reminded him of a narrow, dusty attic there.

At supper Frenchy Blanchette made a point of being agreeable. Gresham, on the other hand, seemed moodily preoccupied. Toward the end Tex said, "I've been thinking, Tony. Maybe we ought to up our offer six-bits a head. I mean to Frank Wagner. That's mighty good cowstuff he's got."

"You mean offer him twenty-seven seventy-five a head? But it's too late. At daybreak he's starting that trail drive to Nevada."

"We could ride over there tonight," Gresham countered. "Twenty-seven seventy-five a head for six hundred twenty-eight cows would come to seventeen thousand four hundred twenty-seven dollars. If we waved a check for that amount under his nose it'd look pretty good to him. Make him think twice before hitting the trail for Winnemucca."

"Ten to one he'd grab it," Tony agreed. "Okay, Tex. Let's saddle up for the Flying A."

In fading twilight they went out to saddle up. "It's a three-hour daytime ride," Gresham said. "Take us some longer at night."

"Just so we get there," Tony said, "before they start south with that trail herd."

As he led his saddled horse from the barn the animal seemed to limp a little. Gresham noticed it too. "Looks like he cast a shoe, Tony."

After a look they saw that the left hind hoof was unshod. Definitely the animal couldn't be ridden fifteen miles tonight on a rocky route. "I'm afraid you'll have to go by yourself," Tony concluded.

Gresham was careful not to assent too readily. "If it was daytime we could drive over in the buckboard, like we did before. But I wouldn't want to try it at night."

"All you've got to do," Tony reminded him, "is wave a check under Wagner's nose. If he turns it down, you tear up the check. If he takes it, you've bought his cows. Let's go up to the house while I write it."

At the house Tony wrote a check for $17,427, payable to Frank Wagner. On the back of it he wrote, "In full payment for 628 head of Flying A cattle and all unweaned calves belonging thereto."

Wagner's endorsement would make the canceled check effectively a bill-of-sale for the chattel purchased.

"I'm betting he'll take it, Tony." Tex Gresham pouched the check, stepped into his saddle, and rode southeast into the night.

Tony slept soundly and in the morning Pedro served him pancakes and eggs. He didn't expect his foreman back till late afternoon.

Just after midday a swarthy rider came

cantering in from the north. The man had a lariat on his saddle horn, big roweled spurs on his boots, a peaked sombrero on his head, and to Tony looked like a typical Oregon cowboy. Frenchy met him at the barn, talked with him briefly, then walked beside him as the man rode on to the house gate.

"I'm lookin' for a saddle job, Mr. Landers. Any chance to get on here?"

"Maybe," Tony said. "I'm letting my foreman pick my crew. He's not here just now. Expect him back before sundown."

Something about the man began to disturb Tony. His mount was a buckskin. There was something else, too, that bothered Tony.

Before he could pin it down Frenchy put in a word. "He's a top hand, all right. I was on the same crew with him myself one time. Forgy's his name. Joe Forgy."

Tony spoke cautiously. "Make yourself at home in the bunkhouse, Forgy, until my foreman shows up. If he okays you I'll take you on."

"Thanks, Mr. Landers." He held a match to his cigarette, then reined his buckskin toward the bunkhouse with Frenchy walking at his stirrup.

All at once Tony knew what the something was which disturbed him. It was the man's voice. Not only the color of his horse but the rider's voice made Tony suddenly sure of his identity.

On the road near Meacham two masked men

had held up the stagecoach. One of them was shot dead by Andy McDowd. The other, who'd escaped on a buckskin horse, was the man who now called himself Joe Forgy.

In a flash of dismay Tony knew he shouldn't have given that check to Tex Gresham. A hollowness at the pit of his stomach warned him that Gresham was off and gone with the check—and that it would never be used to buy Frank Wagner's cattle.

XV

By nightfall Tony was more certain of it than ever. Every hour which passed without Gresham's return served to harden his suspicion. He had a feeling that Frenchy or Forgy, or both, were watching him every minute. Even Pedro the cook could be in on it. It was a definite fact that Forgy was a stage-robbing outlaw.

Had Tony's horse really cast a shoe? More than likely the shoe had been deliberately removed to prevent Tony from making a night ride with Gresham.

In town there'd been talk of an organized gang of outlaws operating in eastern Oregon. A gang directed by a mastermind in Pendleton. Routinely it had robbed stages and driven off livestock—both risky operations. How much simpler it would be if they could steal the value of a large cattle herd by waylaying and cashing a purchase check! All the check needed now was an endorsement by Frank Wagner; an endorsement which could be forged.

Did they have a sample of Wagner's handwriting? Of course! In Gresham's pocket right now was a note from Wagner delivered here by his foreman, Eph Irons.

Would Gresham himself present it at the Portland bank? He might. On the other hand he might double back to Pendleton and turn the check over to some higher-up who would then take care of the endorsing and cashing of the check.

Definitely Tony must get to Pendleton at all costs and from there warn the Portland bank. There was telegraph service west from Pendleton to Umatilla Landing, The Dalles, and Portland.

On that resolution Tony finally went to sleep. In the morning he dressed for a ride to town. Frenchy and Forgy joined him at breakfast and Frenchy said, "Wonder what's holding up Tex. He oughta be back by now."

"Maybe the deal didn't go through," Forgy suggested in a tone of thinly veiled derision. "Could be he's still dickerin' on it with Wagner."

Tony himself couldn't doubt but that Wagner was on his way to Winnemucca on a four-hundred-mile cattle drive which would take several weeks, and during which no one could get in touch with him; and that Gresham, with the check in his pocket, was doubling back north to Pendleton.

"Before you start irrigating today," Tony said to Blanchette, "I want you to put a shoe on my horse." One of the sheds had a forge and an anvil, standard equipment on most cattle ranches.

"I'm not much of a hand at it," Frenchy said. "What about you, Joe?"

"Me neither," Forgy said.

"All right," Tony directed, "then hitch up the buckboard for me. Wanta go to town for a little shopping." Forcing a grin he added, "And there's a girl I want to check on; wanta make sure nobody's beating my time."

The two hands exchanged looks but said nothing. After breakfast they went to the corrals. In a little while Tony saw Frenchy leading a riding horse to the forge-and-anvil shed, as though intending to shoe a hoof. Later Forgy led a buckboard team to a rail in front of the barn, then went back inside for the harness.

It was Frenchy who came first to the house. "They's a few shoes in the forge shed," he reported. "But none of 'em fit your horse. No forge tools, neither; like tongs and hammer. Reckon Pete Carter took 'em away with him."

In a little while Joe Forgy came up with a tongue-in-cheek smirk. "Can't find one of the neck yokes. Anybody know where it is?"

Tony was certain it had all been deliberately planned. The unshod horse, the missing neck yoke, the missing hammer and tongs.

In the kitchen he spoke to Pedro. "You bagged a pair of mallards the other day, Pedro. Think I'll make a try at it myself. Let me have the shotgun."

The cook handed him the shotgun. It wasn't loaded. "Fetch me a few shells," Tony said.

When Pedro pretended to look for shells and didn't find any, Tony knew with dismay that the cook was in it with the rest of them. It had to be that way. Gresham had recruited Pedro. And since it was all a big swindle scheme they wouldn't dare bring an honest cook here.

With little hope of finding it, Tony went to the barn and began a search for the missing neck yoke. To his surprise he found it hidden in a grain bin under some burlap sacks.

The yoke made the harness complete. The buckboard horses were still tied in front of the barn and Tony carried the harness to them. Piece by piece he draped it on the horses, putting a neck yoke on each animal.

The instant the second neck yoke was in place, Blanchette and Forgy suddenly appeared and came at him. At breakfast they hadn't been visibly armed but now each man wore a holstered gun.

"Goin' somewhere?" Forgy challenged.

"Yes," Tony told them. "I just found the yoke you hid in a grain bin."

"You orten't've been so nosey," Forgy said. Just as Clardy had done on the stage road, he walked up to Tony and struck hard with the barrel of his gun.

Again Tony's knees buckled and he staggered back. An old branding iron was leaning against the barn wall and he managed to get a grip on it. As Forgy came at him again Tony swished with the iron and swiped the man across the cheek.

Both men closed in on him and first one, then the other, hit him with his gun barrel.

The world went black for Tony and when he came to his senses Pedro was swabbing his face with a cold rag. The other two men weren't in sight.

When Tony got groggily to his feet the cook left him and he heard the click of a bolt.

His head throbbed and it was minutes before he knew where he was. It was a small, unplastered room with a twelve-inch glassed window at the back of it. Presently Tony went to the window and looked through it. He saw then that he was at a considerable height above the ground.

It made him aware that he was in the attic of the tall Hollister ranch house. He'd explored the attic on his first day here and knew that it had once been living quarters for Glenn Hollister's cook. At the front of it was a sitting room with a pair of dormer windows giving a view of the front yard. Behind the main room was this small sleeping room, on one side of which was a sanitary closet curtained off with canvas. The twelve-inch window in the rear wall gave light and ventilation. It opened on hinges, but would be too small for a man to crawl through.

The door at the front of the room was bolted on the other side. Here there was a cot with blankets, nothing more. In the curtained-off closet Tony found a china pitcher full of water, set in a china bowl, and a tin pail. He looked out the small glassed window and could see the barn, barnyard, corrals, sheds, but not the bunkhouse. Also he could see a cottonwood grove and a strip of creek brush. Blanchette and Forgy were now perched on a corral fence, puffing cigarettes. They were looking up this way, like hounds at a treed cat.

XVI

"Have you been out to look at your Birch Creek ranch yet, Donna?" After a rush of patients Nancy Rollins was having a cup of coffee downstairs at the Delmonico. Donna Costain had joined her there.

"No. And I *do* want to see it," Donna said. "But it's fifteen miles. I can't very well go out there by myself."

"Of course not. The first time I can get a day off, why don't I go out there with you? We could get someone to drive us."

"That would be fine, Nancy. Who could we get?"

Nancy pondered over it. "Doctor McKay's too busy; we might ask Douglas Madigan. But court's in session now and he has a case coming up nearly every day."

Donna had an idea. "I made a friend coming here on the stage. An old Indian-fighter named Josh Bixby. He's still in town. Do you know him?"

"Indeed I do. And I can't think of a better guide than Josh Bixby."

High in the Blue Mountains, in a forest along Shimmiehorn Creek, Kent Durwin stood on his cot to look through a barred window. He'd lost track of how long he'd been here. They'd fed him fairly well and except for a few cuffs at the beginning they hadn't been rough on him. They'd never mentioned Madigan by name. But to Durwin it was fairly clear that he was being held as a whip over Madigan. Unless Madigan "did as he was told," Durwin would be set free on the courthouse lawn at Pendleton.

Tree shadows outside this window told Kent that it was late forenoon. He heard voices from the front room; neither Jody nor Murph had gone out today. He heard Jody say, "I'm gettin' fed up with this, Murph. We're a helluva long way from a barroom."

"We're gettin' paid for it, ain't we?" Murph argued.

The next time Jody spoke his tone had a note of alarm. "Jigger, Murph! Someone's comin'." Then relief replaced Jody's alarm. "It's only Bud Sisters. Maybe he wants Durwin to sign another newspaper."

"It's Bud," Murph agreed. "And he's fetchin' an extra horse. Wonder what for?"

Kent heard the man dismount and enter the cabin. His message was a sharp warning. "We got trouble. Come nightfall, you fellas better skin outa here."

"What trouble, Bud?"

"Sheriff trouble. They raided Chips Kelly's

place. There was gunplay. One of our crew got shot up and five more were jailed. Martin's shakin' 'em down. So far they haven't spilled anything."

"Then why do we have to skin out?"

"They made Chips open his safe and found a sack of money there. Money Ranse Lanagan picked up in a private play of his own at the Villard House. And that newspaper you made Durwin sign. Then they went through Kelly's desk and found a homestead filing. A filing Kelly made two years ago on Shimmiehorn Creek in the Blue Mountains."

"You mean right where we are now?"

"Right where we are now, Murph. So it could give the sheriff an idea; an idea about a hideout where we might be holdin' Durwin. Anyway you got no choice," Bud insisted. "Head man says for you to skin out tonight. He's got a safer spot for you. Do you know where the old Hollister ranch is?"

"It's on Meadow Crik," Jody said, "about fifty miles southwest of here."

"That's right. Ride half of it tonight and hole up tomorrow, then ride the last stretch tomorrow night."

"Who'll we find there, Bud?"

"Blanchette, Forgy, and Archuletta. It's a big house with an attic. Attic's got a room with a lock on it."

"We stow Durwin in the attic?"

"That's it; along with another boy who's already there. You'll need an extra horse, so I fetched one along."

"Maybe we oughta start right now, Bud."

"Better not risk it," Bud warned. "In daylight you'd be seen and reported, likely. Head man says you're to travel only by night."

Presently Durwin heard the messenger ride away. His door opened and Murph brought food in. "Better get some sleep, fella; you'll be forkin' a saddle tonight."

Kent tried to nap but couldn't. What kind of a place was the Meadow Creek ranch? The names Blanchette, Forgy, and Archuletta meant nothing to him.

When the tree shadows were getting long again he sensed an alertness in the front room. "He's heading right this way, Jody!" The alarmed voice was Murph's. "Looks like the same fella who was here before."

"It's him all right," Jody growled. "I can see his badge."

"Name's McDowd. I've seen him around the courthouse. Be nice and polite, Jody, and offer him a cup of coffee."

"He can have anything he wants, Murph, except a peek in that back room."

Kent's door opened. Jody came in with a gun in one hand and tie strings in the other. He made

Kent lie on his stomach while he was tied hand and foot with a rag stuffed into his mouth. "One peep outa you," Jody warned, " 'll add up to two dead men; you and a sheriff who's about to come in."

Jody went out and a bolt clicked. Kent, lying face down, couldn't see anything. In a moment he heard talk.

"Make yourself at home, Sheriff. What about a cup of coffee?"

"No thanks. Is this the claim Chips Kelly filed on coupla years ago?"

"Chips Kelly? Never heard of him. This cabin belongs to an old trapper named Hawkins. Lives at Idaho City."

"I noticed three saddled horses outside. Who's the third one for?"

"Friend of ours from Walla Walla. He's in the back room asleep. When he wakes up we figure to ride over to Meacham."

There was a silence. Durwin could imagine the deputy looking around at signs suggesting preparations for departure; such as blanket rolls all ready for travel. "I'd like to take a look at this Walla Walla man," the caller said quietly.

He had more courage than caution, Kent thought. They were two to one against him.

"Help yourself," Jody said.

"The first thing I'll help myself to," the lawman said, "is your guns." His own was evidently in his hand, covering both Murph and Jody. "Drop your gunbelts and raise your hands. Then one of you unbolt that door and open it."

Kent heard three shots which came almost as one. It meant a shot from the gun of each man and he had no way of knowing which had fired first. He heard someone fall, then for the next half minute, only silence.

The first voice was Murphy's. "Get rid of him, Jody. We can use his horse to load duffel on. I'll start loading up right away."

There was a bustle of movement. Then Murph came in, untied Durwin and led him into the front room. There was no body in sight. Nothing on the floor except three empty cartridge shells and a bloodstain. Outside it was nearly dark. Through an open door Kent saw Jody standing beside four horses. Three had saddles and the other was laden with blanket rolls. "It's a long way to Meadow Crik," Murph said.

XVII

Tony Landers looked obliquely down from his attic prison and saw a saddle horse tied in front of the stable. It was a black horse which he'd never seen till now. Joe Forgy's mount was a buckskin. A newcomer must have arrived on the black within the last hour.

It could be an honest neighbor looking for strays. More likely it was another outlaw sent to join the ones already here. At this midday hour they could all be eating in the kitchen. Tony had been napping on his cot. They brought food to him morning and evening, but not at noon. Once a day Pedro brought fresh water and took away his waste pail. Most of Tony's daylight hours were spent standing at this twelve-inch glassed vent, which overlooked the barnyard.

This was either the sixth or seventh day of his confinement. On every one of those days, from sunup till nightfall, a persistent search had been going on; a search of barn, sheds, corrals, creek brush, and all areas immediately to the rear of the house. A mound of old hay on a shed roof had been forked to the ground and every forkful sifted. Loft hay had been treated the same way. A stack of cordwood had been moved stick by stick and the space underneath spaded up. No regular ranch work had been done. Frenchy Blanchette now used his irrigation shovel to test the ground at various spots. That part of the creek bush which could be seen from rear windows of the house had been beaten through, day by day. Several times Tony had seen Forgy climb a cottonwood tree to pry into a knothole.

Now, unless the newcomer was some honest neighbor, there'd be four searchers instead of three.

When the man went out to his horse, Tony might open his small hinged window and shout for help. He considered the idea only for a moment, then dropped it. It would do no good if the fourth man was another outlaw. If he wasn't, and tried to help Tony, the other three would gun him down.

Witnessing a killing would certainly doom Tony himself. As things stood now, they might merely be holding him until the big check was safely cashed; or until whatever they were searching for was found and made off with. Clearly there'd been two objectives; a raid on the Portland bank account; and the recovery of some hidden treasure.

The first man who came out of the house was Pedro. He went to the black horse, unsaddled it and turned it into the corral. So the newcomer was no passing neighbor. At least he planned to stay for the rest of the day.

When he came out with Blanchette and Forgy, Tony from his high attic vent could see only his back—a man of slight build with bowed, spidery legs. The three walked to the barn and joined Pedro. Forgy took a spade and Blanchette took a rake. Pedro picked up an axe and went into the creek brush. Then the new man came out of the barn with a second spade and stood looking about the grounds, as though undecided where to dig. Now he was facing the house and with a start Tony recognized him. Once before he'd seen that small round face and skinny neck. The man had had one of those spidery legs over a window sill at the Villard House and was making off with money rifled from a woman's underskirt.

There'd been a gun in his hand and his snapshot at Tony had barely missed. The same gun was holstered at his thigh now as he joined Blanchette, Forgy, and Pedro in a treasure hunt. Clearly they had some solid reason to believe that a thing of high value was hidden in or near the Hollister barnyard.

As he watched that day and the next, Tony remembered something else he'd heard about that barnyard. Glenn Hollister had had a prodigal son, Roy, who'd returned from his wanderings, three years ago, housing himself here for a month or so. Then a Kansas outlaw had appeared to confront Roy in a corral which could be seen from this rear window. The two had shot it out, each killing the other—with the charge of "double-crosser" on the lips of the Kansas outlaw.

The shame of it had driven the boy's father back to Tennessee—leaving a sordid theory to be mulled over by Oregon lawmen: that Roy and the Kansan had shared the guilt of a robbery; that they'd buried their loot and separated; that the Kansan had been caught and jailed; that Roy had dug up the money and come west to take refuge on his father's Oregon ranch; finally that the Kansan had escaped jail and followed Roy here to confront him as a double-crosser.

Nothing else made sense. And in some way a gang of Oregon outlaws had reason to believe that Roy Hollister's loot cache was in or near the stable area of this ranch. For these men were looking nowhere else. They searched only on this side of the house. More and more it seemed to be a hurried search. Occasionally Tony heard talk. Once he heard Blanchette say, "Time's runnin' out, Forgy; Ranse says we gotta fade outa here before the . . ."

Tony failed to catch the date of a deadline by which they must "fade out." Ranse was evidently the recent arrival who could have brought orders from the head man at Pendleton. In any case they wouldn't dare stay too long. Ultimately people at Pendleton would hear that Frank Wagner was driving a cattle herd south toward a Nevada rail point. In due time they'd also hear that Wagner had sold his cattle to Tony Landers. The two bits of news would contradict each other and bring the law here to ask why. So Frenchy had good reason to say time was running out.

Another day passed and most of another night. Then, just before moonset, Tony was awakened by sounds of horses and men in the stableyard. He got up and looked from his vent. In the dim night light he saw three mounted men and an extra horse. The men dismounted and Tony saw that one of them was a prisoner. His wrist had been tied to a saddle horn. "You're at the end of the line, buddy," one of the other men told him.

Blanchette and Forgy, half dressed, came from the bunkhouse and joined them. Blanket rolls and duffel were taken from the extra horse. Then all of the men disappeared into the kitchen with the prisoner.

They were still there when daylight came and Tony assumed they were feeding the newcomers, Blanchette probing to find out why the prisoner had been brought here. Only a little later Tony himself found out. He heard footsteps coming up the steep, narrow stairs which led from the second floor to the attic. The footsteps came on across the front room. Tony's door opened and two men stood there. One was Frenchy Blanchette with a gun in his hand. The other was a pale young man of about Tony's own age—gunless, unshaven, and with the fatigue of a long, forced ride printed in haggard lines on his face.

Frenchy shoved him into the room. "You got company, Tony boy." He slammed the door and bolted it on the other side.

The young man who'd been shoved in gave a weary smile and held out his hand. "Sorry to crowd in on you like this. My name's Durwin," he said.

"Mine's Landers," Tony said. "Make yourself at home."

They sat side by side on the cot, sizing each other up—two young, unkempt men who'd never seen each other before.

"Where did they pick *you* up?" Tony asked presently.

"Off a hospital bed. And *you?*"

"Ever hear of a fella named Madigan?"

Kent Durwin gave an open-mouthed stare. "I wish I hadn't. He knocked me on the head and threw me off a bridge. What did he do to *you?*"

"He steered me to a ringer in Jerry DeSpain's office; a phony who claimed to be DeSpain. Listen, we've got plenty of time. Begin at the beginning and I'll do the same."

It took most of the morning for each to get the details of the other's misadventures. They were interrupted only once. Frenchy and Pedro unbolted the door, Pedro coming in with an extra cot and blanket, Frenchy with a cocked gun. The only words came from Frenchy. "There'll be two of us every time, from now on."

When they were gone Tony said, "Means they won't let Pedro come up by himself, after this. They'd be afraid we might jump him and grab his gun."

"I'd sure like to get my hand on one," Kent said.

"Let's talk about Madigan. From what you say, they've been using him for a hole card to make him do jobs for them. What job's he doing for them right now?"

"Murph and Jody talked about it," Kent remembered, "these last two nights when we rode here from the mountains. Seems a saloonman named Chips Kelly was picked up in a raid, along with five or six other toughies. But Kelly's the only one who knows the dirt on Mr. Head Man, whoever he is. Mr. Head Man's afraid Kelly might turn state's evidence unless he's acquitted at a trial coming up pretty soon. So he's making Madigan defend Kelly in court. Madigan doesn't want to, but there's nothing he can do about it."

Tony nodded. "And it could be they need Madigan to help them cash a check I wrote. They've got him pulling strings for them. When he's pulled his last string, we're a cinch to be bullet bait, both of us."

"That especially goes for me," Durwin agreed.

"Because I heard Murph and Jody fire the shots that killed a deputy named McDowd."

"Which brings us back," Tony summed up, "to question number one. How do we get our hands on a gun?"

A dozen times during the day they weighed the hazards of jumping Pedro and his backer the next time the door was opened. Always they came to the same conclusion. "It'd be a suicide," Durwin agreed.

In the evening when Pedro came with food and water it was Jody who stood back of him with a gun. Jody, who'd shot down Deputy McDowd at the Shimmiehorn hideout.

"I can tell on him," Kent reminded Tony when they were alone again, "if I ever got to town, so he'll make sure I don't get there."

"I can tell a few tales myself," Tony added grimly. "So they'll make sure I don't get anywhere either. They're just waiting till they get that check cashed; and until they've made the Pendleton lawyer jump through his last hoop."

Light faded outside and they lighted their candle. For an hour they sat in its dim glow mulling over the single hopeless alternative to doing nothing at all. "Let's sleep on it," Tony said finally. "Maybe one of us'll get a better idea before morning."

Tony's better idea came well after midnight.

Durwin, wearied from two straight nights in the saddle, was sleeping soundly on the other cot. What impressed Tony was the stillness of the house.

If the six men were in lower-floor rooms there'd be an occasional sound. A footstep in a hallway, a voice, or an occasional cough. Suddenly it occurred to Tony that they'd logically be sleeping in the bunkhouse. They'd eat at the main house, a common practice at many ranches, but it would look unnatural to a passerby if six saddle hands were sleeping in the family bedrooms of the owner's residence. A passerby or a stray man from another ranch, might happen along at any time. For the sake of appearances Frenchy's crew would want to make themselves look plausible under any such inspection. So more than likely all six of them were asleep in the bunkhouse from bedtime till breakfast.

All but Pedro. Pedro, as a cook, would get up an hour earlier than the rest. He'd come to the main house, fire the kitchen stove, and start making breakfast.

Was there a way to lure Pedro into coming up here alone? It was worth a thought. No use waking Durwin yet. Let him catch up on sleep.

A plan came to Tony and he got up to prepare for it. First he lighted a candle. Next he wrapped his right hand in a blanket and used it to smash the pane of glass out of the twelve-inch window.

Then he took down the canvas curtain which served as a door to the wash closet. It gave him a rectangle of light canvas or duck cloth about three by six feet.

He picked up the biggest segment of broken glass and began using it as a cutting edge. With this piece of glass it was slow and awkward. But he had plenty of time. And he only needed to make a slight slit in the upper edge of the canvas. With that as a start, he was able to rip a full-length strip from it—a strip six inches wide and six feet long.

With infinite patience Tony repeated this ripping until he had six stout strips of duck cloth, each about six inches wide and six feet long. When he tied them together, end to end, it made in effect a rope about thirty feet in length.

He weighted an end of it and let the weighted end out the open vent, and when the line was all paid out he tied the top end to a window hinge. The lower end would now be at or near the ground, not far from the kitchen door.

The angle of the moon told Tony it lacked only an hour or so of dawn. He let Durwin sleep a little longer, then shook him awake. "Keep your fingers crossed, pardner. I've just baited a trap."

Kent sat up drowsily, blinking at the lighted candle. He saw glass fragments on the floor. "What's up?"

"Take a look outside and see."

Durwin went to the open window and put his head through it. Looking down he saw dimly, in the starlight, what seemed to be a knotted rag rope reaching to the ground.

He turned with a puzzled stare. "But what good is it? You know damned well you can't squeeze through that hole. And neither can I."

"That's right," Tony agreed. "If I could, I'd've been gone long ago. But stop and think a minute. Six men are asleep in the bunkhouse. By all rights, the cook'll get up an hour earlier than the rest of them. He comes to the kitchen door, sees a rope hanging from our window, so what does he do?"

Kent continued to stare. "I'll bite. What *does* he do?"

"He thinks we wouldn't go to all that trouble for nothing. He wonders if the vent's maybe a little bigger than he'd thought. He probably never measured it. He's only seen you twice, Durwin. Maybe you're a little skinnier than I am. Only one of us would need to go down that rope; then he could run up two flights of stairs and unbolt the door. The cook listens. Everything's quiet; no one stirring up here. So I ask you again, pardner; what does he do?"

Kent's eyes narrowed as he caught the logic of it. "He might run up for a look, just to make sure we're here."

"And if he does, we take him. Him and his gun.

The corral's got horses. The barn's got saddles. If it works out that way we could have a fifty-minute start."

Tony blew out the candle and the two sat in the dark, waiting. A fifty-minute start would take them a long way toward Pendleton.

XVIII

When the darkness outside changed to thin gray they heard footsteps coming from the bunkhouse. Kent picked up the heavy china pitcher and stood just a little to the left of the door. Tony, barehanded, took the same position at the door's right. If opened, the door would swing into the attic's front room.

Anyone coming in wouldn't be able to see them until he was at least halfway through the doorway. The cook's only purpose in coming would be to make sure there'd been no escape. At first glance this rear room would seem to be empty. The cook would have a gun in his hand. Before he could use it a china pitcher would crash on his head and Tony, from the other side, would be snatching at the gun.

It would work only if Pedro came up here alone.

They heard him arrive at the kitchen door. There the footsteps stopped. It meant that he'd seen the hanging rope. He'd be looking up at the open attic window from which the rope hung. Would he run to the bunkhouse and waken the others?

For more than a minute no further sound came from below. Pedro would be standing there, puzzled. The gray square of window space was now a little brighter. It was time for the cook to make his breakfast fire. But first he must find out the meaning of this hanging rope.

Tony and Kent stood rigid, silent, backs to the wall, straining ears for the next sound. Then, from two floors below, they heard a door open and close. The kitchen door. Pedro had come inside—which meant that he wasn't rushing off to raise an alarm at the bunkhouse.

Now they could hear him coming upstairs. His steps arrived at the second-floor hallway and stopped there for a moment. Then they came on up the second flight to the attic. The footsteps crossed the attic's front room and stopped just outside this bolted door.

Without unbolting the door Pedro called out, "*Levantese*! Time to get up, you in there. I have your breakfast."

The man waited for an answer while the prisoners stood breathless. The cook repeated his call, this time in a coaxing tone. "Wake up, in there. I bring cakes and coffee."

Another minute of silence. Then the sound of a bolt sliding back. The door swung slowly into the other room. Kent and Tony couldn't see Pedro nor could he see them. The man would be looking into gray dawn light and would see two empty cots. Also he'd see that the duck cloth curtain was gone from in front of the lavatory—and the open vent from which the rope hung. That and nothing more. His gaze would fix in absorbed speculation on the open vent. Was it humanly possible for a grown man to squeeze through it?

The first thing Tony saw was the muzzle of a gun. It came halfway through the doorway and for a moment came no further. The next sound from Pedro was an exclamation in Spanish— "*Carramba! Se fueron!*" To Tony from Tennessee it meant nothing. To Kent Durwin from Colorado it meant—"Damnation! They're gone!"

When the gun came another few inches through the doorway they could see the hand which gripped it. Then a forearm; then a face in profile. Durwin banged the china water pitcher down on Pedro's head just as Tony snatched at the man's gun hand.

Only one syllable of alarm came from Pedro. His next was smothered by another clout on the head from Durwin. Then Tony Landers had the gun. Between them they battered Pedro to the floor and dragged him to one of the cots.

Kent crammed a rag in his mouth while Tony pulled in the hanging rope. They used it to tie Pedro securely, wrists and ankles.

They left the cook helpless there and went out, bolting the door. Tony, with Pedro's gun, led the way down to the bedroom floor. The only room they searched was the one which had been used by Tex Gresham. All he found was a box of 44-40 rifle shells. With these he hurried on downstairs. "Look for anything that shoots, Kent."

The lower floor had no rifle or revolver but in the kitchen they found Pedro's shotgun and in a cabinet they found a box of twelve-gauge shells. Tony stuffed the shells into his pockets. "Head for the barn." Tony led the way there on a run.

Saddles were draped on saddle trees in the barn vestibule. One of them had a scabbard with a carbine in it. Yesterday there'd been three horses in the corral. The other mounts had been turned out to pasture. "We pick the best two and saddle up, Kent."

The best two were a rawboned buckskin and a rangy bay. After slipping bridles on them they opened the corral gate and chased the third horse out.

Kent used the saddle with the carbine in its scabbard. Tony was tying the shotgun to his saddle strings. In a minute more they were loping upvalley.

Presently they rounded a bend of the brushy stream and were screened from sight of the house.

Durwin pulled to a walk. The horses hadn't been fed this morning and would be easily winded. But Frenchy's crew, when they discovered the escape, wouldn't take time to feed theirs either. First they'd have to catch the loose wrangle horse. Then the several other mounts would have to be brought in from pasture.

The trail crossed and recrossed Meadow Creek. Tony watched for landmarks, trying to remember just where they'd struck this stream when he'd come here with Gresham and Pedro.

"Seems to me it was about here." He reined to the right, away from the stream, and headed northwest toward a notch in a ridge.

Halfway up the slope the unfed mounts began lagging, stopping rebelliously now and then to snatch at weeds and high grass. "If we push 'em they'll play out on us," Kent warned.

At the next grassy glade he called a halt and both men dismounted, "We better let 'em rest and feed awhile, Tony."

They took the bits out of the horses' mouths but left the headstalls on. "Half an hour of it'll put 'em in shape again," Durwin calculated.

Tony, impatient to be moving on, looked back over the route they'd traveled. The sun was just beginning to peep over the skyline of the Blue Mountains.

"Without Pedro to wake 'em up," Kent hoped, "maybe they overslept a little."

The first man up, Tony reasoned, would go to the house for a cup of coffee. He'd wonder why Pedro wasn't in the kitchen. Then he'd look out and see an empty corral. It wouldn't be long until he'd run to the attic where he'd find Pedro tied up—and the prisoners gone.

He'd speedily arouse the others. On foot it would take them a little while to catch up the wrangle horse, still longer to bring in mounts from the pasture.

"Let's walk the rest of the way up," Kent suggested. He began walking, leading the bay, followed by Tony leading the buckskin.

It took them another hour to reach the notch. "From here," Tony said, "we've got a water grade all the way to Pilot Rock."

But Kent was looking back over the route they'd come. What seemed to be five moving dots were coming this way.

Tony followed his gaze and both men knew it was pursuit. "Am I counting right?" Durwin wondered. "Oughta be six of 'em."

"More likely five," Tony argued. "They'd likely leave Pedro behind. What we're looking at now is Jody, Murph, Blanchette, Forgy, and Lanagan."

"We're half an hour ahead. Let's go."

They rode down the west slope of the ridge and presently came to willow-lined Pearson Creek. "About six miles down this," Tony remembered, "will take us to East Birch Creek. And about ten miles down East Birch'll take us to Pilot Rock."

"Which reminds me," Kent said, "that about four miles before we come to Pilot Rock we'll hit the old Costain ranch. That's where I got the deadwood on Madigan. Only I didn't know it was Madigan."

"Now you know it was Madigan," Tony agreed, "because when you told him about it he socked you on the head and threw you in the river."

He kneed his mount and Kent kept pace with him. The junction with East Birch Creek wasn't yet in sight.

"We could be on the Umatilla Indian Reservation now," Tony guessed. "Likely the first house we'll come to'll be the Costain cabin."

"Which is empty," Kent reminded him. "But it's got four stout log walls in case they catch up with us about there."

A nine-point buck jumped from the brush and ran ahead of them with high, zig-zagging bounces. Looking back Tony couldn't see the pursuers. By now Frenchy's crew should have topped the ridge and be coming down into this valley; but timber would hide them if they were more than half a mile away.

"Just how much deadwood have we got on them?" Kent speculated.

"From what I know and what you tell me," Tony summed up, "we've got murder on Jody and Murph. We've got fraud on all the rest of them plus murder of the Costain family on the Pendleton lawyer; not to mention him dropping you off a bridge."

"And Tex Gresham, who slickered you into

writing a fat check. Wonder if he's cashed it yet."

"I don't see what's to stop him," Tony worried. "It's good at the bank and the bank knows my signature; it says the check's payment for a herd of cattle and the bank knows that's what the money was put there for."

By the angle of the sun it was midmorning when they came to East Birch Creek. Here there were big, leafy cottonwoods as well as wild fruit thickets. They forded to the right bank and headed downstream.

"Six miles to the Costain cabin, pardner," Kent calculated, "and four more to Pilot Rock. If our broncs don't founder we'll make it."

But only a few minutes later he looked back and had doubts. Five riders were in sight and gaining. "Maybe we didn't pick the best mounts after all," Kent muttered. When he tried to force his horse to a run the nearly spent animal rebelled and kept to a walk.

"They've got spurs and we haven't," Tony said.

Tony untied the shotgun from his saddle strings and Durwin took a carbine from its scabbard. "If they catch up, Tony, we'll hunt cover and shoot it out."

But the only cover in sight were trees in which they'd quickly be surrounded.

Again Tony looked back and this time he made out the leading pursuer, Joe Forgy. Forgy was a bare quarter mile behind them and would soon be within rifle range. "Only chance we've got is to hole up in the Costain cabin."

The next time Tony looked back he saw that Frenchy Blanchette had caught up with Forgy. The other three pursuers were strung out behind them.

Far ahead Kent Durwin saw a grove of big cottonwoods which looked familiar. "It's the Costain place, I think." Before Kent could say more a rifle cracked and a bullet whistled overhead.

"Don't shoot back, Tony. It'd slow you up and you wouldn't hit anything." Kent used the stock of his carbine to club his mount into a run. Tony Landers, clubbing with the stock of his shotgun, managed to keep up.

Another bullet whizzed by and Kent, looking back, saw that the rifleman was Forgy.

"There she is!" Tony shouted. He pointed ahead at a building layout—log cabin, barn, and sheds. No sign of life showed there and the stone chimney was smokeless.

They were in the grove now and for a moment were screened from the sight of pursuers. Kent jumped from his saddle, rifle in hand, and ran the last forty yards to the cabin. There he fired a bullet through the door lock, then kicked the door open.

He dived inside and Tony Landers, with a shotgun, was right back of him. As they slammed the door a bullet splintered its panel.

A minute later shots were coming from more than one direction. Windowpanes were shattered. Bullets came singing into the house and plunked into plaster walls. Kent looked over a sill and saw Forgy, still asaddle, pumping lead from a range of a hundred yards.

From another side came the voice of Blanchette. "You've got no water in there, boys. You'll be wantin' a drink pretty soon. Come on out to the well and get it."

"Circle from window to window," Kent advised, "Shoot once with that shotgun just to let 'em know you've got it. After that, don't shoot unless they rush us."

Tony looked at the short tree shadows and knew that it was about noon. Maybe someone from Pilot Rock would ride this way and hear the shooting. Otherwise it seemed hopeless. The men outside had five rifles and as many holster guns—and were sure to have more ammunition. Tony had Pedro's revolver in his belt but no extra shells for it.

Another rifle slug smashed through the door panel. Only a few inches from Durwin's elbow a bullet chipped plaster from an inner wall. He saw Murph aiming a carbine from the barn door. Kent took a snapshot and the man ducked out of sight.

Then a hail of shots came from the opposite side of the cabin. Kent heard an answering blast from Tony's shotgun. "I had to, Kent," Tony called out. "Two of them were charging the kitchen door. Jody and Lanagan. I dropped Lanagan and Jody pulled him back behind a shed."

A grim memory came to Kent Durwin. "Know what it reminds me of, Tony? Reminds me of two years ago when they thought Indians were raiding this same cabin. Shooting out windows and plunking slugs into the logs. Only it wasn't Indians; just a crooked white man trying to make it look that way."

He shifted to the next window and peered over its sill. Half of Joe Forgy's face showed from back of a cottonwood bole. Kent fired and chipped bark there. From somewhere else another rifle cracked and Kent felt a burn at his cheek. It left a bloody streak. As he dodged to one side he thought again of Madigan.

Madigan, who'd started it all—just two years ago at this very cabin.

XIX

Tony's shotgun boomed again from a back window. "I shouldn't have. He wasn't close enough."

"Who was it?"

"Jody. He yelled something that made me mad; so I cut loose."

"What did he say?"

"He asked what I'd trade him for a pail of well water."

Kent thought it over glumly during the next hour when no firing at all came from the besiegers. "They won't need to smoke us out. They can just keep us penned up till we keel over."

"Looks like our only chance," Tony said, "is for somebody from Pilot Rock to happen by. Anyway I think Lanagan's out of it; maybe he's dead."

The long quiet outside seemed endless to Kent. Yet he knew by the length of a tree shadow that it was still only midafternoon. Warned by what had happened to Lanagan the outlaws were playing it safe. *Waiting us out,* Kent concluded, *instead of shooting us out.*

Tony tried to ease the tension. "How'd you like a nice, juicy pork chop, Kent? Along with a cool glass of buttermilk to wash it down?"

Kent circled the windows and on this round he

didn't even see a besieger. "They're waitin' till dark, Tony, so they can sneak up on us."

He kept circling and on his next round he glimpsed Joe Forgy. The man was in the barn loft peering from the hay door. Kent's quick bullet made him dodge out of sight. Then a fusillade of six fast shots from a repeating rifle came from Tony's side of the cabin.

"It's Jody again," Tony reported. He didn't fire back.

There was another nerve-wracking quiet and then an amazing letdown. It came suddenly and Kent could hardly believe it. First he saw Frenchy Blanchette, who'd made his way afoot to a spot east of the cabin, in the open and just out of rifle range. Frenchy was staring off toward the northeast with a look of alarm. Apparently he saw someone coming from that direction which Kent, from a cabin window, couldn't see.

All at once Blanchette turned and sprinted for the horses, shouting to the others. As he came within range Kent fired twice and his second shot made Frenchy stumble. He scrambled to his feet and went on, limping. "A leg hit, I think," Kent said as Tony joined him. "They've got the wind up, somehow. Frenchy saw someone heading this way—someone he'd rather not tie into. Look; they're joining Frenchy at the horses."

The horses were slightly beyond fair range but Kent sprayed a magazineful of bullets that way.

Trees partly obscured the group there. Four men mounted horses and Frenchy Blanchette, with a bullet-bit leg, picked the nearest one, which happened to be Forgy's buckskin. At once the four made off into upcreek timber.

"Lanagan isn't with them, Tony. So you must've nailed him. Who do you reckon they saw coming? Let's go see."

"Wait," Tony cautioned. "Might be a trick to get us outside. We're not sure Lanagan's dead. If he's not he could pick us off."

"Don't I hear wheels?" Durwin cupped his hand to an ear. "Wagon wheels?"

In a minute distinct wheel sounds could be heard approaching from the direction of Pendleton.

A two-seated buckboard turned into the grove. The driver had a gray beard. "Whoa there!" he called to his team. "Here we are, ladies."

In the back seat were two lovely young girls with parasols. A tall, dark-haired girl and a slighter one with bright yellow hair. Tony knew both of them but Kent Durwin knew only one. The girl they both knew worked in Doctor McKay's office. The other had arrived in Pendleton on a stagecoach with Tony Landers.

And so had the rig's grizzled, wind-blistered driver, Josh Bixby.

Kent forgot his shaggy, blood-smeared face as he ran out to them. Tony was only a step behind.

"Nancy!" Kent exclaimed. "You shouldn't have come—they might have . . ." He stopped when he realized she didn't recognize him. A rifle was still in his hand and Tony still had his shotgun. The next word came from Bixby. "What the heck's goin' on around here!"

"You're Tony Landers!" Donna Costain said in shocked surprise. "We thought you were down on your ranch!"

Kent managed a grin. "Reckon we look like a coupla wild men. We've been on short rations. Better not come too close. Last bath I had was at the Villard House."

Then Nancy knew him. He looked twenty pounds underweight and had the hairiness of a tramp. "We thought you were dead!"

"You didn't miss it far," Kent said as Josh Bixby got out and handed Nancy from the rig. Donna jumped down without help. Then Tony recovered his wits and gave a warning. "Better get inside, everybody. I don't think those fellas'll come back—but they might. They've been gunning hell out of us."

"You mean we scared 'em away?" Bixby said. "Me—I didn't even bring along a gun."

"But they didn't know it," Kent explained as he herded them all into the house. "You were too far away. All they could see was a buckboard with three people in it. They had to make a fast choice—either kill you or run."

Bixby gave a grim nod. "So they ran. Sheriff gave you up for dead, boy, after he sent someone to find out why Andy McDowd didn't come back from the Shimmiehorn. They found McDowd near a hideaway cabin with a couple of slugs in him—and signs that a prisoner had been held there by two men." His gaze shifted to Tony Landers. "How'd he come to hook up with you, boy?"

All the concern at Pendleton had been for Durwin, none of it for Tony Landers.

So it was Kent who had to answer most of the questions. While the girls drew him out, Tony took Bixby aside. "One of those men didn't get away," he whispered. "Let's take a look."

They found Ranse Lanagan back of a tool shed. The charge from the twelve-gauge shotgun had struck him frontally and he'd stopped breathing. "Best the girls don't see him," Tony decided; and Bixby agreed.

"I better get the four of you down to Pilot Rock," Josh said. "They got a hotel there. You can stay all night and go on to Pendleton in the morning."

"Trouble is," Tony objected. "I've got to send a telegram right away; to a bank in Portland."

"Leave that to me," Josh offered. "Soon as I get you to Pilot Rock I'll light out for Pendleton by saddle. Write your telegram and I'll file it. And I'll tip off Sheriff Martin. Just what does he need to know?"

"Tell him that Douglas Madigan knocked Kent Durwin on the head and dropped him in the river. Did it because Kent found out he killed the Costain family two years ago."

Tony touched only the high spots. He could report the details in person when he got to Pendleton. Right now they moved Ranse Lanagan and his guns into the tool shed. "We'll send a man out here from Pilot Rock," Bixby said, "to ride herd till a coroner shows up."

When they got back to the cabin, Durwin had brought a pail of water from the well. Nancy Rollins with the deft touch of a nurse was bathing the bullet nick in his cheek.

"Josh," Tony told them, "wants us to head for Pilot Rock and stay all night there. What do you say, Kent? A bath, a shave, a fried chicken supper with two pretty girls across the table . . ."

"You've sold me," Durwin broke in.

"Soon as you're safe there," Bixby promised, "I'll burn leather for Pendleton and get a manhunt started. Miss Costain, you'll have to inspect your ranch some other time."

No one argued with him. Donna was gazing around at the shot-out windowpanes and at scraps of shattered glass on the floor; and at the bullet-pitted walls. "They say it was like this two years ago," Nancy told her, "right after an Indian war party raided your uncles. Only Doctor McKay said it wasn't Indians." Her gaze shifted to Kent

Durwin. "And you, Kent, said Doctor McKay was right."

"I was guessing then," Kent admitted. "But I'm dead sure of it now. Tell you all about it on the way to Pilot Rock."

In a few minutes he was holding the reins of the buckboard team with Nancy on the front seat beside him. Tony and Donna had the back seat while ahead of them Josh Bixby rode Kent's horse, leading Tony's. It was nearly sundown and the girls no longer needed their parasols. There'd just be time, Kent estimated, for a bath and a shave before supper. After that a night of sound sleep on a real bed. Nancy more than anyone else insisted on that. "You're both terribly exhausted and undernourished. So consider yourselves my patients till I turn you over to Doctor McKay."

Kent clucked to his team while Tony, on the back seat, resisted an urge to slip an arm around the slim shoulders of the girl beside him. The arm was too ragged and dirty.

"How," she asked him, "did you like your Meadow Creek ranch?"

"Just fine, Donna." It was an inadequate answer but the right one would have to wait. He couldn't tell her now that the ranch lacked only one charm—herself, to help him make a home there. The wheels bumped along slowly as they moved on down the fringe of creek brush toward the village of Pilot Rock.

XX

The daily stage from Umatilla Landing was due in Pendleton and Sol Olcutt, waiting for it, made himself comfortable in the Villard House lobby. He sat facing the Main Street window which overlooked the sidewalk on which stage passengers would disembark. If all had gone well, Tex Gresham would be one of them and he'd have a satchel full of money from a Portland bank.

And what could have gone wrong? Gresham was no ordinary cowhand. He had looks, a certain dignity, and anyone would take him for a successful stockman. There was no way for a Portland banker to know that Frank Wagner, a Camas Prairie stockman changing from cattle to sheep, was now driving his cattle on a long, slow trail to Winnemucca, Nevada. When a rangeman with the personality of Tex Gresham, calling himself Frank Wagner, presented a check clearly signed by Tony Landers, with the check's purpose inscribed on its back in the handwriting of Tony Landers, apparently endorsed by Wagner, why would the bank turn it down. Turning it down might offend and repel two potential accounts, Landers' and Wagner's.

What made Olcutt confident that all had gone

well was that there'd been no telegram to the contrary. There was wire service from Portland to Pendleton. In case of refusal, Gresham had been instructed to send Olcutt a three-word message: "FRISCO OFFER ACCEPTED." It would mean that Gresham was catching a boat for San Francisco to avoid prosecution for attempted fraud.

No such message had come. Out on the walk a group had assembled to watch the stage come in. It had left Umatilla Landing eight hours ago, just after the arrival there of a Columbia River sternwheeler from Portland.

"There she rolls!" a man shouted; and now Olcutt heard a rumble of wheels coming up Main. In a moment the four-horse team was pulled to a halt by driver Tom Vaughan, directly in front of Olcutt's window.

The last passenger to get off was Tex Gresham, dressed in corduroys, boots, and a cattleman's hat. The bag he carried was small—but plenty big enough to hold eighteen thousand dollars.

Through the windowpane his eyes briefly met Olcutt's. Gresham smiled, gave a faint, affirmative nod, then disappeared down the Main Street walk.

Olcutt left quietly by the Court Street door and hurried to the Walla Walla Club. Daylight was fading as he went up to the gaming rooms. These he by-passed as he took a private hallway to Max Charny's private office at the rear.

Charny was waiting for him. "He's in," Olcutt announced in a tone of triumph. "Bag and all."

"We've been overdue for a break," Olcutt agreed, "and now we've got one. Soon as it's dark, Tex'll fetch it to us."

Gresham, they knew, would come in by an alley door and slip up to this office. Until now, none of the gang except Olcutt had been allowed in the Walla Walla Club. When in Pendleton they'd always assembled at Kelly's Maverick Bar. But the Maverick had been raided and was now boarded up, front and back. Kelly himself was in jail and awaiting trial. The smartest lawyer in town, Douglas Madigan, at Charny's command would defend Kelly in court. It was the best Charny could do to placate Kelly, who otherwise in bitterness might turn state's evidence.

There'd been many holdups, stock raids, barroom rollings, and swindles this past year, with Charny in the background pulling strings. Of the Maverick Bar heelers, only Kelly could tell tales on him. Only Sol Olcutt had an open connection with the Walla Walla. In extreme emergencies Gresham and Blanchette had sometimes reported here for orders, but only after dark by the alley stairs.

Up those stairs, from the gloom of night, came Gresham with a bag of money. Olcutt let him into the office and locked the door. "It went over smooth," Tex reported as he tossed the bag on the desk. "Count it."

Charny dumped out packets of currency. In all it came to seventeen thousand, four hundred twenty-seven dollars.

"Any trouble, Tex?"

"None at all, Max." Gresham helped himself to a cigar. "It was all set up for me. They'd already cashed eight or ten of Landers' checks, good as gold. Next check was due to be for the cows themselves—and this was it. Cashier was expecting it. The money had been put there by Glenn Hollister for just that purpose."

Charny counted out a thousand dollars, handed it to Olcutt. "Your cut, Sol." He gave another thousand to Gresham. "And yours, Tex."

"What about Frenchy and the others?" Gresham questioned. "They're due five hundred apiece, ain't they?"

Charny nodded. If he believed in anything at all, it was that you must never double-cross the help. If you made them sore they'd get even, one way or another.

Now he made six piles of money with five hundred dollars in each pile. He put them in six envelopes and labeled the envelopes: "Blanchette"; "Jody"; "Murphy"; "Lanagan"; "Forgy"; and "Archuletta." "Pass them out, Tex, when you get back to the ranch."

Gresham agreed and pouched the envelopes.

"Okay, Max. But we dassent stay there too long."

"Which still gives you two or three weeks," Charny said, "to look for the Roy Hollister money."

"I'll go along myself and help," Olcutt offered. "It's bound to be there. The letter the boy wrote to his wife says he could see it from his bedroom window."

"Everything oughta be safe for the next three weeks," Charny reasoned. "It'll take that long for Wagner to drive his stuff to Winnemucca."

"What about Landers?" Gresham asked the question with small relish and took the answer with even less. Under his skin he was a little softer than either Charny or Olcutt.

"Get rid of him," was Charny's blunt verdict. "And Durwin along with him. Turn 'em over to Joe Forgy."

It was all he needed to say. Forgy was the executioner. When a witness had to be eliminated, he was usually turned over to Forgy.

"Anything else, Max?"

Charny couldn't think of anything else. Nor could Olcutt. They had no way of knowing that at about dawn this morning two prisoners had escaped from an attic.

The first intimation of it came barely a cigar puff later with the sound of footsteps coming up the back stairs. When Olcutt unlocked the door

Frenchy Blanchette burst breathlessly into the office.

He was limping and there were bloodstains on his pants leg. "Hell to pay, Max!" he blurted. "They got away from us—both of 'em. We chased 'em clear to East Birch Creek, where they made a stand at the old Costain place. We were smokin' 'em out of it when we seen a rig comin' and had to back off. Means they'll be in town talkin' to the sheriff before morning."

Charny was a gambler. All his life he'd played for big stakes and this wasn't the first time he'd lost a jackpot. He knew how to take a sudden unexpected loss and he took this one with barely a blink.

"Where's Forgy and the rest of them?" he asked calmly.

"They're hightailing for the Payette River hideout in Idaho. All but Ranse Lanagan. I had to come in to tip you to what happened—and to pick up what's coming to us. Five hundred apiece, you said."

Charny cocked an eye. "Why all but Lanagan?"

"He's dead. One of those boys had a shotgun and blasted him."

Charny turned to Gresham and held out his hand. Tex took an envelope from his pocket, the one labeled "Lanagan." He passed it to Charny, who removed the money from it, adding it to his own pile. No use paying off a dead man.

"I'm beat up; me and my bullet-chipped leg," Frenchy said. "What about me holing up here till tomorrow night? Foundered my horse gettin' here and I'll need a fresh one; and a bandage on this leg. It's two hundred miles to the Payette River hideout."

Charny nodded. Frenchy, exhausted and with a bad leg, was in no shape to start a long, punishing ride tonight. "Tomorrow night'll be soon enough," he agreed. "And Sol, you and Tex'll have to go with him. Everyone but me has to clear out. Tonight and all day tomorrow the three of you can lie low at the Maverick. It's boarded up, front door and back. The law raided it, searched it upstairs and down—so they won't search it again. There's a window catch loose at the back. Get in there and go to bed upstairs. Keep quiet till this time tomorrow night. By then I'll have three strong fresh horses waiting right back of it."

Sol Olcutt too was a gambler and knew how to lose. He gave a shrug of compliance. It had to be a fadeout for everyone but Charny. For Olcutt, who'd posed as Jerry DeSpain. For Gresham and Blanchette, who were up to their necks in the Meadow Creek ranch fraud.

But Charny himself had left no tracks. His hand had guided everything, but it didn't show. Neither Durwin nor Landers had reason to accuse him. They'd point fingers at everyone else, including

Madigan. Most of all at Madigan. And only Madigan would be picked up. Would he stand pat and deny everything? Or would he crack up and implicate Charny?

"We better not take any chances," Charny decided. "And time's short. By midnight this thing'll break wide open." He looked from Olcutt to Gresham to Blanchette. Gresham was the shrewdest, he knew, but the man with the coldest blood in his veins was Olcutt. Charny picked up the five hundred dollars which would have been the share of Ranse Lanagan. "This is for you, Sol. You can earn it in about ten minutes on your way to the Maverick."

"What doing, Max?"

"Stop by Madigan's cottage at the corner of Willow and Webb. The sheriff'll be calling on him before morning. So you better get there first."

Olcutt understood. He took the money, then went out with Gresham and Blanchette. Charny was glad to be rid of them. By this time next week they'd be safe at the Payette River hideout in Idaho. No reason for the law to look for them there; or even at the Maverick, which had already been searched and sealed.

Charny snuffed out his cigar and went forward into the barroom. His red-haired hostess was perched on a bar stool and he joined her there. "It's a dull night, Max," she said.

"Maybe things'll pick up before morning, Helena." Charny looked wistfully at her exquisite profile and wished he was fifteen years younger. Would she ever consent to marry him? And would the law ever find out that she was the widow of a spoiled juvenile named Roy Hollister?

XXI

A pounding on his door wakened Sheriff Martin. He sat up drowsily, lighted a lamp, and saw that it lacked half an hour of midnight. As the thumping continued the sheriff put on pants, slippers, and a robe. When he opened the door he was surprised to see an old-timer named Josh Bixby. A hard-ridden horse stood by the gate. "Hell's to pay, Bill!" Josh announced. "That boy Durwin just turned up, alive and kickin', with a tale of devilment that'll burn your ears off."

Bixby, Martin remembered, had left town this morning in a buckboard with two young ladies. "Durwin! Devilment! What's goin' on, Josh?"

"Tell you about it while you're strappin' yer gun on, Sheriff." Bixby stepped inside. "First off, we gotta send this telegram."

More and more confused, Martin lighted a lamp and read the message which Bixby handed him.

> The Willamette National Bank,
> Portland, Oregon:
> Stop payment on check for $17,427; endorsement forged.
>
> Tony Landers.

Martin looked up, mouth open. "Landers? I thought you said Durwin."

"I did. It's both of 'em. They're at Pilot Rock restin' up after a man-killin' ride and a shoot-out. How many handcuffs you got, Sheriff? You'll need plenty of 'em. First pair'll be for Doug Madigan."

While Martin finished dressing Josh Bixby kept up rapid-fire talk. "It was Madigan who knocked Durwin on the head and dumped him off the bridge. Did it because Durwin found out he'd shot up the Costains two years ago. He . . ."

"Say that again, Josh." Sheriff Martin, half-dressed, stood gaping while Bixby said it again. And more. To Martin it seemed wildly incredible.

"Sol Olcutt's in on it too," Josh insisted. "He made believe he was Jerry DeSpain and . . ."

That was too much and Martin broke in with a snort. "You're crazy! How could Olcutt pass himself off for DeSpain? They're as different as I am from a Piute sheepherder."

"But young Landers had never seen either of 'em," Josh explained. "So when Madigan introduced Olcutt as DeSpain . . ."

"Let's get back to Durwin," Martin broke in. By now he was fully dressed, with a badge on his coat and gunbelt at his waist. "You say he found a post-office box key buried along with those Costain rifles? Which key was it?"

"For Box Number Sixty, Durwin says."

It was the one point which impressed Martin. He happened to know that Douglas Madigan had always rented Box Number 60 at the local post office. Unless Durwin was telling the truth, how could he know that box number? "Maybe Doug can explain it," the sheriff muttered. "Anyway he has a right to know what he's bein' accused of. Let's go have a talk with him."

They went out and walked down Willow Street. On the way Bixby kept adding details. One of them couldn't be denied. For Deputy Andy McDowd *had* been found shot dead in the Shimmiehorn Creek cabin.

"From there," Bixby kept insisting, "they took Durwin fifty miles to the Meadow Crik ranch where they penned him in the same attic with the Landers boy. That was to give Tex Gresham time to cash a check at Portland. So we'd better be sendin' the telegram to stop payment . . ."

"It's too late, Josh. Gresham was seen getting off a stagecoach this evening with a handbag. So if what you say is true the check's already been cashed."

They passed the Hollister town house, now occupied by Judge LaDow, and went on to the cottage used by Madigan.

Martin went to the cottage door and knocked. When there was no answer he tried the door. It was unlocked. "If he's home we'll wake him up, Josh. If he isn't we'll sit down and wait."

They groped their way into the dark parlor. "Hi, Doug!" Martin called. "Sorry to bother you this late but . . ." He stopped when his foot bumped into something which wasn't furniture.

Bixby struck a match. In the flare they both saw Madigan. The man lay on the floor, motionless, and even in the dimness they both sensed that he was dead. Bixby's hand shook a little as he lighted a lamp. The man on the floor was coatless and there was blood on his shirt. Martin touched him and found the flesh still warm.

"Did someone gun him?" Bixby asked hoarsely.

"Looks like a knifing," Martin said. "Not more 'n an hour or so ago, looks like." After a closer inspection he added, "Neighbors might hear a gun so someone just hit him on the head and finished up with a knife."

Getting grimly to his feet the sheriff of Umatilla County could no longer doubt the report sent in by Kent Durwin.

It took him a full hour to mobilize his deputies and alert the county coroner. Just after one o'clock they all assembled in Martin's courthouse office.

"We got a peck of trouble," he told them, "and some of it won't wait till morning." In as few words as possible he relayed the information given him by Bixby.

"Which starts us out," he finished, "with two dead men. There's likely to be a few more before we get through."

"I'll go roust out Peabody," Coroner Lindsay grumbled. "Nate can have Ranse Lanagan while I handle Madigan." Doctor Nathan Peabody sometimes acted as deputy coroner.

When Lindsay went out Martin faced his own deputies, Bob Sargent, John Sperry, and Alvin Fox. Fox had lately been appointed to replace Andy McDowd. "Look high and low for Tex Gresham," Martin ordered sharply. "He got here from Portland on the evening stage, probably with a bag of money. Likely he divvied it with Sol Olcutt. Olcutt meets the description Tony Landers gives of a man who impersonated Jerry DeSpain. Check the livery barns. Take a look in every bar and hotel and rooming house. I'll go over to the Walla Walla Club and if Olcutt's there I'll pick him up. First thing in the morning I'll get off a telegram to the Portland bank."

Sargent was senior deputy. "John," he directed, "you take one side of Main and let Alvin take the other. Double back up Cottonwood and don't overlook Chinatown. I'll take the hotels and rooming houses."

They hustled out, and Sheriff Martin went alone to the Walla Walla Club. In the gaming rooms he found some forty customers. Max Charny circulated among them, suave and smiling. At the bar Harry Jarboe of Heppner was trying to promote himself with the club hostess.

Martin drew Charny aside. "Where's Sol Olcutt?"

The gambler raised his eyebrows. "How did you know, Sheriff?"

"How did I know what?"

"Sol resigned, all of a sudden, about five hours ago. He didn't say why. Took me by surprise. Whatsamatter? Is Sol in trouble?"

"Up to his neck." Martin gave Charny a searching look. "And so are you, Max, if you're hiding him somewhere."

"Me?" Charny managed a hurt look. "You know I wouldn't do that, Sheriff. What's going on, anyway?"

"Fraud, for one thing. Murder for another. Someone paid a call on Doug Madigan and left him dead on his parlor floor. And not long ago Sol Olcutt made out like he was Jerry DeSpain. Turns out Madigan was in on that. It ended up with Tony Landers getting gypped out of seventeen thousand dollars."

"The devil you say!" Charny's tawny eyebrows raised still higher. "First I heard about it. Anyone else in on it?"

"Tex Gresham, for one. You know Gresham?"

"Heard of him. Top hand on some cow ranch, ain't he?"

"Claimed to be. Mind if I look around, Max? I don't have a search warrant but I can get one."

"You don't need it, Sheriff. Help yourself."

Charny led Martin from room to room. Olcutt wasn't hiding in any of them. "If he was in some bunco game with Gresham," Charny insisted, "they didn't cook it up here."

There was no way to prove it wasn't true. Nothing in the reports of Durwin and Landers implicated Charny. "Olcutt must have a room somewhere," Martin prodded.

"Sure. He kept a sleeping room at the New England Hotel."

Martin rattled off a list of names: Jody, Forgy, Murphy, Blanchette, Archuletta. "They used to hang around the Maverick Bar. Any of them been in here?"

Charny looked insulted. "We don't cater to that class of trade, Sheriff."

Martin went out and hurried to a small hotel called the New England. There was no night clerk. The sheriff punched a bell which summoned the elderly proprietress.

"Sol Olcutt has a room here. I want to see him."

"He's gone," the woman said. "He came in about ten o'clock, packed a bag, paid his bill, and checked out."

"Did he have a horse tied in front?"

"I didn't notice."

"I'll have a look in his room, please."

She led him to a room at the back of the ground floor. Most of Olcutt's effects were still there.

Apparently he'd packed in a hurry. Several abandoned suits hung in a closet and Martin went through all the pockets.

There was no money or anything valuable. But in an inner pocket of a coat the sheriff found a letter. It had been written at Knoxville, Tennessee, and was addressed to Jerry DeSpain of Pendleton, signed by Glenn Hollister, and introducing his nephew Tony Landers.

It verified the confidence conspiracy described by Landers. With his jaw squared grimly the sheriff went out to join his deputies in a townwide manhunt for Gresham and Olcutt.

By breakfast time neither man had been found. Jaded by the search, Martin met with Sargent and Fox at the Delmonico Restaurant. Josh Bixby joined them there. "You boys rounded up anybody yet?"

"Nobody but Max Charny," Martin admitted glumly, "and we can't pin a thing on him."

"We've shaken down every livery barn, saloon, and rooming joint in town," Sargent reported. "Nobody's seen Gresham since he came in on the stage."

Bixby asked, "What about that telegram, Sheriff?"

"I just filed it," Martin said. "Not that it'll do any good. If Gresham had failed to cash that check he wouldn't've come back at all." He showed them the letter of introduction he'd found in Olcutt's room.

Sargent nodded toward the street door. "Here comes Sperry. Looks kind of excited. Turn up anything, John?"

"I turned up a saddled horse," Deputy Sperry reported as he joined them. "A buckskin with a few bloodstains on the left stirrup leather. Abandoned at a hitchrail. Might've been standin' there all night. Ben Gray saw it and took it to the Pioneer barn."

"Hold on a minute," Josh Bixby broke in. "A buckskin, did you say? I recollect somethin' the Durwin boy told me. Said the last shot he fired was at Frenchy Blanchette. Said it made Frenchy stumble and then limp on to the nearest horse; which happened to be Joe Forgy's buckskin. Said it looked like a leg hit and Frenchy needed help to get in the saddle."

"Even if it was only a flesh scratch," Martin concluded, "it would bleed enough to stain a stirrup leather. And now that I think of it, they wouldn't all take off for whatever hideout they're headin' for. They'd need to send one man into Pendleton with a tip-off for Sol and Gresham; let 'em know about Landers and Durwin gettin' away. Give 'em a chance to get to hell out of here before those two boys show up in town."

The reasoning was solid. "Yeh," Bob Sargent added, "and with a bullet-nicked leg Frenchy

Blanchette would be the one to come in. He'd be in no shape for a long ride to Idaho, or Nevada, or wherever they're heading for, until he could get that leg patched."

"Olcutt could patch it for him," Martin said, "and get him a fresh horse. So it's three men we're looking for, instead of only two. Olcutt, Gresham, and Frenchy Blanchette."

XXII

The road from Pilot Rock to Pendleton followed down the east bank of Birch Creek and then veered to the right toward lower McKay. This morning Kent Durwin again held the reins of a buckboard team with Nancy on the seat beside him. Again Tony was on the back seat with Donna Costain. This morning Tony, with a clean, scrubbed look, felt bold enough to drop an arm around Donna's shoulders. She smiled up at him.

"It was a shame to wake you boys up," Nancy Rollins was saying, "after what you've been through."

There was no great reason to hurry, since a full report had been sent in last night by Josh Bixby. "They'll have Olcutt and Madigan locked up by this time," Tony said confidently. "And maybe Gresham too."

Donna spoke to Kent Durwin. "Do you still want to buy my ranch?"

"I sure do," Kent told her. "Half down and the other half on time."

"Sold!" Donna agreed promptly. "How soon do you want to move in?"

"Just as quick as I can patch over the bullet holes and put in new windowpanes. Lots of things'll need fixin' up. Maybe I can get you to help me, Nancy."

"We'll both help him, won't we, Donna?" Nancy evaded. Kent hadn't asked her to marry him yet but she knew it was coming.

The buckboard rattled on along a trail which had now left Birch Creek and was angling northeast. Presently they came to a wooden bridge over McKay Creek and drove across it.

Late in the morning they came to the south end of Main Street in Pendleton. As Durwin trotted his team up saloon row, curious onlookers watched them from both sides. There were barroom idlers, shoppers, stockhands, here and there a blanketed Indian. Some yelled questions, a few cheered, most of them merely stared. Evidently by now the entire town had heard the highlights of the report brought in by Bixby.

One saloon they passed, The Maverick, had boards nailed across the door. Its window shades were drawn and no sound came from it.

At Webb Street the sidewalks began and from here on the hitchracks were full. Wagons, saddle horses, ranch rigs, and town buggies lined the street on both sides. "There he is!" a man shouted. "The fella Madigan chucked off the bridge. I sure never figgered to see *him* again!"

"There's that kid from Tennessee too!"

When they'd dropped Nancy at the Hollister Block and Donna at the Villard House, Tony and Kent hurried to look up Sheriff Martin. As they crossed the courtyard, mention of Douglas

Madigan stopped them with a shock. Madigan, they learned for the first time, had been murdered in his cottage parlor early last night. "Reckon he knowed too much," an idler said. "So they shut him up."

Kent and Tony found Martin in his office. Kent reported first, adding a few details to what Josh Bixby had already brought in. Tony added a few more details. Both had to admit that they'd never heard the outlaws mention the name Charny. "Head Man was all they called him," Tony said. "I figured they meant Olcutt."

"We just got an answer," Martin told them, "from the Portland bank. Our wire got there too late; they'd already cashed the check. Looks like Gresham came in with the money on the stage yesterday evening and divvied it with Olcutt. We can't find them anywhere in town so they must've taken off with it. Frenchy rode in with a bloody leg and warned 'em—chances are all three of 'em are forty miles away by now."

Two reliable men, Tony learned, were on their way to the Meadow Creek ranch. "One of them," Martin said, "will pick up Pedro if he's still there; but it's likely the cook has lit out by now. Other man'll take care of your stock, Landers, till you get back there."

Tony grinned. "All the stock I've got are two teams and a guernsey cow. And no money to buy any more. That last big check cleaned out my balance at the bank."

"You saved this, anyway," the sheriff said dryly. He handed Tony his uncle's letter of introduction to Jerry DeSpain. "The real Jerry DeSpain's in his office right now."

"We'll be at the Villard House if you need us," Kent said.

Martin looked up sharply. "I'll want you both here at three this afternoon. Judge LaDow and the county attorney'll be on hand. We'll get you boys to sign statements. Mostly it'll be a strategy meeting to figure out just where we'll go from here."

"Okay, Sheriff. See you at three o'clock." They left the courthouse and went gratefully to their rooms at the hotel.

There was just time to freshen up before meeting the girls for lunch. Almost at once their table was surrounded. A man from the *East Oregonian* was there, firing questions, taking notes. Others swarmed up, congratulating Tony and Kent, welcoming them back to Pendleton.

Afterward they went into the hotel parlor, hoping for privacy but instead being invaded by a parade of well-wishers. It was like an informal, spontaneous reception—the friendly and the merely curious from town and country crowding in. Among them was Doctor McKay who stood beaming as he shook hands with Kent Durwin. "I always said it wasn't Indians, young man, who raided that ranch; but you're the first to back me up on it."

As three o'clock approached Town Marshal Gray came in to remind Kent and Tony of their appointment at the courthouse. They hurried over there and found eight men assembled in the sheriff's office. Besides Martin and three deputies, there were County Attorney Henry Yoakum, Judge William LaDow, Deputy United States Marshal Thad Unger, and a man named Crago who'd just arrived from Pilot Rock.

Crago was reporting: "I found hoofprints where four riders took off southeast from the East Birch Creek cabin."

"Four of them," Martin interrupted, "were shooting up the cabin when Josh Bixby's rig drove in sight; so everybody but Frenchy took to the hills while Frenchy came in to tip off Olcutt."

"Halfway across the reservation," Crago reported, "they came onto a band of Indian ponies. Drove 'em ahead of them a piece and then rode through 'em, scattering 'em. No way to tell which tracks is which."

The sheriff nodded. "But chances are they kept on heading southeast."

"Toward Idaho," Deputy Sargent agreed.

The country attorney had a frustrated look. "So where does that leave us?"

Marshal Unger spoke to Tony Landers. "While

you were at the Meadow Creek ranch, did a federal agent named Whitcomb ever come by looking for a pair of horse traders? They're wanted for selling whiskey to Indians."

"Never saw or heard of them," Tony said.

"Whitcomb disappeared," Unger explained, "not long ago. His horse was found grazing loose along Bear Wallow, about halfway between your ranch and Albee. Understand you and Gresham attended an auction sale at Albee. Did you go home together?"

"No," Tony remembered. "I went ahead and Gresham followed with the stuff we'd picked up at the auction."

"Could be," Unger brooded, "that Whitcomb ran afoul of Gresham. We know he didn't catch up with the traders. Maybe . . ."

He was interrupted by a knock at the door. A timid knock, barely audible.

Martin looked toward Deputy Sperry. "See who it is, John."

When Sperry opened the door, the striking young woman who stood there was well known in Pendleton. A tall, slender redhead of stunning looks—but just now her cheeks had no color and her eyes were clearly frightened. As she came in she looked over her shoulder as though fearful that she'd been followed.

Ten men stared at her.

The county attorney was the first to speak.

"Anything on your mind, Helena?" She made certain that Sperry had closed the office door. Then she spoke in a low, taut voice. "Is it true that they killed Mr. Madigan?"

"That's right," Martin affirmed bluntly. "Which one of 'em did it, Helena?"

"They didn't need him anymore—so they killed him." She stated it as a brutal fact, naming no names.

"He knew too much, did he?" Martin coaxed.

Again she looked nervously at the closed door. Then in a thin voice she went on, "I know too much too; so why won't they do the same with me?"

After a silence Attorney Yoakum said gently, "The way to make sure they won't is for you to help us put them behind bars."

Deputy Sargent drew up a chair for her. She sank into it and covered her face with both hands. Then she looked up pleadingly. "Will you protect me, please?"

"We certainly will," Yoakum promised.

"What I want," Helena told them, "is an escort to Portland who'll see me safely aboard a steamship for San Francisco."

Judge LaDow said gravely, "I'm sure that can be arranged, Miss."

"My name," she corrected, "is Mrs. Helena Hollister."

XXIII

A clerk was called to take down her story.

"What we need to know most, and first," Martin prompted, "is where their last ditch hideout is. Got any idea about it?"

"They never confided in me," the Walla Walla hostess said. "But during three years at the club I sometimes heard bits of talk I wasn't meant to hear. I think they have many places to hide—but the one they depend on most is on the Payette River."

"Yeh?" Martin prompted keenly. Everyone in the room knew that the Payette River was in Idaho. "Where abouts on the Payette?"

"I think it's just a little way above where it comes into the Snake," Helena said. "They spoke of an old adobe farmhouse with a red barn back of it."

"We'll find it all right. And we'd better not lose any time." Martin turned to his senior deputy. "Bob, get started for Idaho right away. It's in their jurisdiction and so they're the ones to raid that hideout. You can pitch in and lend 'em a gun hand, if you like."

U.S. Deputy Marshal Unger stood up. "I'll go along with you, Sargent," he decided. "Fugitives crossing from Oregon into Idaho puts 'em in *my* jurisdiction too."

They all knew that the Snake River made the boundary between the State of Oregon and Idaho Territory. The stage road to Boise City crossed it at Weiser, and a short way above Weiser the Payette River joined the Snake. "Tell the Weiser sheriff," Martin cautioned, "that he'll need a plenty big crew to smoke those fellows out. Jody, Murph, and Forgy'll get there a little before you do. On your way."

Deputy Sargent hurried out with Marshal Unger.

"Go ahead, Mrs. Hollister," Judge LaDow prompted gravely.

"I married Roy," she told them, "in Wichita, Kansas. He kept bad company but I never knew what they did. Except that suddenly Roy disappeared and three months later I got a letter from him. It was sent from Oregon. He said he was at his family ranch on Meadow Creek, and that he had a lot of money. The money was hidden, he said, where no one but him could ever find it—a place he could see from his bedroom window. He asked me to join him at Pendleton."

"So you went by train to Kelton, Utah," Yoakum suggested, "and from there you rode a stagecoach to Pendleton."

"No," Helena said, "I went by train to San Francisco and from there by steamer to Portland. Then by riverboat to Umatilla Landing. But when I got to Pendleton I learned Roy was dead."

"It fits," Sheriff Martin agreed. "About that time he and a Kansas outlaw named Wasco killed each other at the Hollister ranch. We looked up Wasco's record and found that he and another man had made off with a fifty-five-thousand-dollar railroad payroll. Seems they buried the money and split up; later Wasco was caught and jailed. Still later he broke jail. We doped out that the second man was Roy Hollister; we figure Roy dug up the money and took cover at his dad's Oregon ranch. Wasco followed him there and they shot it out."

"The letter," Helena insisted, "said nothing about that; only that Roy had money hidden where he could see it from his window, and for me to join him."

Martin nodded. "So when you got here he was dead; which left you stranded."

"I'd spent my last cent getting here," Helena said. "At Wichita I'd worked as hostess in a gambling place and it was the only way I knew to make a living. So I went to the Walla Walla Club and asked for a job. Mr. Charny took me on—and ever since then he's been coaxing me to marry him."

"Why didn't you?" Yoakum queried.

"Because I despise him," she said quietly. "There was another reason. I'd married one outlaw and I wasn't going to marry another."

"Did you show him the letter from Roy?"

"No. But he searched my room and found the letter."

Martin took a look at his notes on Tony's report. "So from your attic peephole you saw Gresham's crew searching the barnyard. Go ahead, Helena."

"Max Charny," Helena told them, "is undercover owner of a cheap saloon called the Maverick. I don't really know anything about what went on there. Except that in a place like the Walla Walla you hear lots of talk. The Maverick was mentioned as a hangout for toughs and outlaws. Max Charny never went there and he never allowed any of the Maverick people to come to the Walla Walla. He used a man named Bud Sisters to carry messages back and forth."

Martin turned abruptly to John Sperry. "Did we pick up Sisters in that raid the other day?"

"No, we didn't," Sperry said. "Sisters didn't happen to be in the place when we hit it. That's why he's not in jail right now."

"I saw him," Helena revealed, "just about an hour ago."

"Where?" the sheriff demanded keenly. "At the Walla Walla?"

"He came slipping in by the back stairs," the hostess said, "and I heard Charny give him an order."

"Yeah? An order to do what?"

"He told Sisters to get three strong fast horses and have them grained. Just after dark tonight

Bud is to take them to a vacant lot behind the Maverick Saloon."

The sheriff looked at her and his jaw dropped. The same sheepish expression came to the faces of his deputies. The Maverick! The place they'd raided, searched, closed, and boarded up, after jailing Chips Kelly. It was the only place in town where they hadn't looked for Olcutt, Gresham, and Blanchette.

Martin came out of it and whacked fist into palm. "Charny would count on us not looking there. Empty and sealed up like it is. So it was the very spot for him to hide them!"

"Frenchy, with his bloody leg!" Sperry agreed. "They can lay low there till dark tonight, then hit for Idaho on fresh horses. What are we waiting for, Sheriff?"

XXIV

Deputy Sperry was impatient to lead a charge on the Maverick but Martin held him in leash. "Let's get organized first, John. Olcutt and company won't try to leave cover till night time. First man we need to pick up is Charny. We want to take a look in his safe. What about a search warrant, Henry?"

"It won't take but a few minutes." The county attorney exchanged nods with Judge LaDow and both men left the office to prepare the warrant.

"I'll recruit six men from the street," Martin decided, "and deputize them. Three can go with me to pick up Charny." He turned to Deputy Alvin Fox. "You take the other three, Alvin, and raid the Maverick joint." He took a key from a desk drawer and tossed it to Fox. It was a key to the boarded-up front door taken after the earlier raid. "While you're doing that, I'll ask Ben Gray to make a round of the bars and pick up Bud Sisters."

A protest came from Sperry. "That leaves me out, Sheriff. Which raid do I get in on?" Now that Sargent had been dispatched to Idaho, Sperry was the senior deputy.

Martin answered him by calling attention to Helena Hollister. "We promised her an escort to

Portland and safe conduct aboard a ship there. Your job, John. As soon as she signs a statement about the Walla Walla, take her to a room at the Villard House and post a guard outside her door. Then order a private conveyance. When it's ready you can drive her to Umatilla Landing and then both of you can ride a riverboat to Portland."

The assignment disgruntled Sperry but he knew better than to argue. The argument came from Kent Durwin. "What about Tony and me joinin' up with Fox's party? Frenchy and company handled us pretty rough—and we'd like to have a crack at 'em."

Martin shook his head. "You're in no shape for it. Oughta be in bed, both of you. Anyway we don't need . . ." He stopped as a thought struck him. Tony Landers, the Tennessee boy, wouldn't be much help in a close-up gunfight.

But Durwin was a Colorado cowboy. He'd be handy with a belt gun and could be counted on to strengthen the Maverick raiding party.

"I want Landers to stay out of it," the sheriff decided. "But Durwin, if you want to you can get yourself a gun and go along with Fox. Here we are," he added as Yoakum came in with a warrant for searching the Walla Walla Club.

After checking the warrant, Martin stuffed it into his pocket. "Everybody stay right here till I get back." He went out to recruit and deputize six dependable citizens.

• • •

Half an hour later three of those dependable citizens, along with Kent Durwin, left the courthouse with Alvin Fox. Simultaneously three others went out with Sheriff Martin, heading for the Walla Walla. Fox's party hurried toward the Maverick. Helena Hollister was in a room at the Villard House under the protection of John Sperry.

Fox's crew included a hard-bitten ex-stage driver named Rawson, a ranch hand from the lower Umatilla named Brody, and Josh Bixby. Two of the party carried tools for ripping boards off a door.

When they came to Chips Kelly's place it showed no sign of life. "Bixby, you and Rawson and Durwin'll bust in from the back. Brody and I," Fox directed, "will go in at the front. Make it four o'clock on the dot." It lacked only a few minutes of four.

Durwin circled to the alley with Bixby and Rawson. Rawson had a pry bar. The boards nailed across the alley door were still firmly in place. But Bixby's keen eye saw a broken window catch. Hideaways could have entered by that window.

When Rawson's watch said four o'clock he slipped his pry bar behind one of the door boards.

As he ripped the boards off sounds from the front meant that Alvin Fox was doing the same thing. A minute later they heard Fox and Brody charge into the barroom. No resistance in the barroom meant that it was unoccupied. None was expected. Logically three hideaways would be in sleeping rooms upstairs.

There was a click as Deputy Fox unbolted the alley door from the inside. Bixby, Rawson, and Durwin followed him through an empty kitchen into the barroom. At the foot of stairs leading upward from the barroom stood the cowboy Brody with a cocked gun. Nothing but silence came from above.

"But they're here all right, three of 'em." Josh Bixby pointed to the bar on which the others at first saw nothing. Except for a thin layer of dust the bar surface seemed to be bare.

After a closer look Kent made out four small circles in the dust; four rings in a row. One was about two and half inches in diameter and the other three only a little more than an inch. "A quart bottle of whiskey and three jiggers," Bixby explained. "They helped themselves to a drink before going upstairs."

Fox joined Brody and shouted up the stairs. "Come on down, Sol; you and Gresham and Blanchette. Toss down your guns first."

Still only silence from overhead. Had something warned them of an impending raid? It was barely possible that Sisters, the go-between, had seen Helena go to the courthouse and had rushed here with a warning.

"Nothin' we can do," Fox decided, " 'cept go up there after 'em."

The stairs were just wide enough for two men to ascend abreast. The gray-haired Bixby moved forward to take a stand beside Fox.

Riser by riser, guns drawn, the two began the ascent. Brody and Rawson followed, three treads behind. Kent was close back of them. There was a bend in the stairs halfway up. They rounded it without challenge. After that they could see part of the upper hallway.

Fox knew the second-floor layout. "Three sleeping rooms on the right; two and a washroom on the left. Long straight hallway in between, with a window at each end."

His nod beckoned the others on. Still no sound came from the sleeping rooms.

"We'll start at the front room and take 'em one at a time," Fox said when all five of them were at the top.

Then he raised his voice to shout, "We're givin' you one more chance, Olcutt. Five to three against you."

Still only a dead quiet. The five raiders moved forward along the hall to the front. There Fox kicked a door open and exposed an empty bedroom.

It was the same with a room on the opposite side of the hall.

But in the room next to it the bed had been

slept in. Also a sheet had been taken from it and torn into strips. The unused strips still lay on the floor. "It's where they wrapped up Frenchy's leg," Bixby concluded.

They looked into one more empty room and again found a slept-in bed. And now Kent heard a sound from one of the rearmost rooms. Fox heard it too and raised his voice. "Last call, Sol. We know you're there—you and Gresham and Frenchy Blanchette."

Another sound came from the back room and Josh Bixby identified it. "Someone just opened a window; an alley window and they're skinnin' out of it."

"Okay," Fox muttered. "Two of you better take a look."

Bixby hurried downstairs with Kent Durwin at his heels. They raced out into the alley and when they looked up they saw an open window. The two men who'd dropped from it were now running across a weed-grown lot.

"Slow up!" Bixby yelled as he fired at them. It was a miss, but close enough to make the pair turn and shoot back.

Durwin felt the breath of a bullet from Tex Gresham as he began tripping his own trigger. At his elbow Bixby missed again and then stumbled. A bullet from Olcutt had broken his arm and another from Gresham splintered the kitchen door.

Kent could hear firing from the upper hallway. Blanchette, with a sore leg, would be cornered up there. In the vacant lot he saw Gresham fall face down and out of sight in the high weeds. Olcutt had turned and was almost out of range when Kent let go with the last bullet in his gun.

It dropped Olcutt in the weeds there.

Then Alvin Fox was calling from the upper window. "Frenchy shot it out with us, all by himself. He winged Rawson but we've got him tied up now."

"I'm the lucky one down here," Kent reported. "Josh has a busted arm. Olcutt and Gresham are both down."

He advanced into the weeds and found Gresham with a bullet-smashed rib. Olcutt had taken a head hit and was dead.

It was sunset by the time Bixby, Gresham, Rawson, and Blanchette had been taken to the McKay clinic and Olcutt had been turned over to the coroner. Kent went with Deputy Fox up a noisily excited Main Street hunting for Sheriff Martin. They found him at the county jail, where he'd just locked Max Charny in a cell.

"Roundup's over, Sheriff," Fox reported. "And look what we found on 'em." He took four envelopes and a handful of loose currency from his pockets and dropped them on a desk in the jail office. "Adds up to an even five thousand."

Martin sat down and looked at the envelopes. Each had a name written on it: the names *Jody*, *Forgy*, *Murphy*, and *Archuletta*; and each envelope held five hundred dollars. "We took it off Tex Gresham," Fox explained, "after Durwin gunned him down."

"Payoffs due those four buckos," Martin concluded, "whenever Gresham could join 'em at the Payette River hideout."

When he counted the loose currency it came to three thousand dollars. "Fifteen hundred was on Olcutt," Fox revealed, "an even thousand on Gresham, and five hundred on Frenchy Blanchette."

Martin said, "These are new banknotes issued by the Willamette National of Portland. I picked up some more just like 'em at the Walla Walla Club."

"In Charny's safe?" Kent prompted.

"No. Money in the safe was old bills, gold dust, and silver. Nothing else in the safe except that letter of Roy Hollister's that his wife told us about. Backs up her story all right. But when we frisked Charny's bedroom we found a trunk with a false bottom. Cracked it open and found money. Guess how much."

"About twelve thousand," Kent guessed.

"Let's be accurate," Martin said with a smile. "It came to twelve thousand four hundred twenty-seven. When we add what you boys brought in from the Maverick . . ."

"It makes exactly what they cashed Tony's check for," Kent exclaimed with a lilt of elation. "So Tony gets every dime of his money back and can still buy himself a herd of cows."

"The only losers," Martin summed up, "are the Charny-Olcutt-Gresham gang. It's a cinch Frank Wagner doesn't lose anything. Right now he's halfway to Winnemucca with no idea he's been used as a blue chip in a swindle."

Town Marshal Ben Gray came in prodding a prisoner in front of him. "Bud Sisters," he reported. "Picked him up at the Webfoot. Where'll I stow him, Sheriff?"

"We've got a full house, Ben. You'll have to slap him in the same cell with Chips Kelly."

Kent Durwin laid his gun on the office desk. "I won't need this anymore, Sheriff. Right now I'm off to tell Tony he'll get his money back."

Tony wasn't in the courthouse. But in the Villard lobby Kent found Donna Costain. When he told her about recovering the Portland bank money she joined him in a search for Tony.

"Maybe Nancy knows where he is, Kent." But when they went up to Nancy's reception room at the McKay clinic, Nancy had no idea where Tony was. She herself was busy helping three doctors treat casualties brought in from the Maverick gunfight.

From there Kent and Donna went down one side of Main and up the other. The last place they looked was the post office and there Lot Livermore remembered seeing Tony. "Passed him over on Willow Street a while ago. He was sitting on that stone carriage block in front of Judge LaDow's house."

"What on earth would he be doing there?" Donna puzzled as she hurried with Kent to the corner of Willow and Alta Streets.

Tony, still sitting on the carriage block, hailed them with a grin.

"What's the idea?" Kent asked curiously.

"I'm waiting for Ed Fuller," Tony told them. "I sent word to him to fetch along a hammer and a wrench and a can of oil."

Kent gave a confused stare. Ed Fuller was a blacksmith with a shop only a block from here.

Then it dawned on Donna that the big, two-story house on this corner was part of the Glenn Hollister estate. It had been the family town house used by the Hollisters during the days when Tony's uncle had operated the ranch on Meadow Creek.

"That scamp cousin of mine, Roy," Tony reminded them, "showed up at the ranch with a bag of payroll loot, remember? He wrote his wife he'd stashed it in a spot he could see from his bedroom window. But Roy wasn't the kind to spend much time on a ranch. Ranch life would bore him silly. He'd like town life, saloon life, the bright lights, a lot better. So he'd put in a lot of his time in Pendleton. No use for him to go to a hotel when his dad owned the best house in town. So it makes sense to figure he'd sleep in it whenever he came to town."

Kent began to catch the drift. "Got any idea which room he used?"

"I just knocked on the door," Tony told them, "and asked Mrs. LaDow if she could help me out on that. She and the judge moved in right after the Hollisters left here. I asked her if she'd found any sign as to which room had been used by Roy."

"Had she?"

"She remembers finding a pair of dice in a dresser drawer of an upstairs front bedroom. My uncle's a strict churchman; he never touches dice or cards. So that front upstairs room must have been Roy's. It overlooks the street. So when Roy wrote Helena that he could keep an eye on his money from his room window . . ."

"You mean he buried it in the front yard?" Kent broke in. "Or slipped it under that carriage block you're sitting on?"

"Maybe," Tony said. "More likely it's in that hitch post. The head screws on. But the threads are rusted tight so it'll take tools to get it off. Here comes Fuller now."

The brawny blacksmith and his helper came up with tools—an anvil hammer, a pipe wrench, and a can of lubricating oil.

The hitching post was a three-inch cast-iron pipe with a cast-iron horse's head screwed on the top of it. "See if you can get the head off," Tony said.

It didn't take long. A few hammer blows, a few twists with a wrench, and a lubrication—and then the head began to turn. When it came entirely off an upright hollow cylinder five feet long and three inches in diameter was exposed. Money was in there—some of it in currency and some of it in gold coin.

What else could it be but the Kansas payroll money? "Kinda wraps everything up," Kent Durwin agreed. "The Charny gang had the right idea—but the wrong house."

XXV

Aspen parks in the Blue Mountains had turned from olive green to red gold when wedding bells rang at the Garden Street church in Pendleton. Snowfall hadn't yet begun and the Umatilla River, at its lowest stage of the year, now riffled placidly under the Main Street bridge. It was high noon and rigs from town and country lined the street. People streamed into the church, women in their best Sunday bonnets and men spruced from their polished, spurless boots to white, winged collars. Every seat was full when the local schoolteacher, Amy Brundage, sat down at a small, treadle organ and began playing.

The bridegrooms, with a solemn little preacher standing between them, had already taken places at the front. From an anteroom off the vestibule, under the belfry, came the brides. A tall, stately dark-haired girl and a delicate little blonde with matching veils and floor-length gowns. In slow cadence they came hand-in-hand down the aisle and all of Pendleton loved them.

They separated at the foot of the aisle, Kent Durwin claiming Nancy and Tony reaching his hand to Donna Costain. The organ music stopped and the double ceremony began.

In the midst of it two in the front pew stood

up to take part; the county's most distinguished surgeon to give Nancy Rollins in marriage; and an older man to give Donna. In a too-tight frock coat borrowed from Doctor McKay, Josh Bixby performed his office with a proud dignity. He was Donna's oldest elderly friend in Oregon; in his day he'd driven stagecoaches and whacked bulls, but this, with his gray beard neatly trimmed and a glow on his blizzard-scarred face, was the high moment of his life.

When it was over the only reception was a crush of felicitations as the two couples moved up the aisle. Then they were outside, where it was only a short block to the cottage which Nancy had shared with Amy Brundage. There the brides went in to change while Tony and Kent, surrounded by well-wishers, waited by a rig tied in front.

It was a one-seated rig, for only the Tony Landers were leaving town today. When Donna came out dressed for travel Tony handed her into it. Kent Durwin gave him a house key. "Make yourselves at home, out there."

Nancy had a last word with Donna. "You'll find everything you need out there, for tonight."

She meant that the log house on East Birch Creek had been refurbished and refinished, its floors scrubbed, its windowpanes replaced, its bullet-pitted scars plastered over. But Kent, who'd purchased it from Donna Costain, had to be a star witness in Judge LaDow's court day after tomorrow. So he was loaning the house to Donna and Tony, who'd use it as an overnight stop on their way to Meadow Creek.

There was a chorus of good-byes and a shower of rice. Then Tony drove off and out of town, taking the Pilot Rock road.

Presently the road left the Umatilla River and angled southwest toward the McKay Creek bridge. "A shame," Donna said, "that Nancy and Kent can't go home right away. It won't be very romantic staying at the Villard House."

"For them it will." Tony whipped up his team again.

"How long will the trial last?"

"Only a day or two, let's hope. With Kent as a witness they'll make short shift convicting that pair."

In a showdown gunfight at the Payette River hideout, in Idaho, there'd been only two outlaw survivors. Murph and Jody. They'd been brought back to Pendleton for trial, charged with the abduction of Kent Durwin and the murder of Deputy McDowd.

"Soon as it's over," Tony added, "Nancy and Kent can set up housekeeping at the East Birch place."

"I didn't see Sheriff Martin at the wedding, Tony. Was he there?"

"No. He's on his way to Salem with three

prisoners." The Oregon State Penitentiary was at Salem and three of the Walla Walla Club conspirators—Charny, Gresham and Blanchette—had been sentenced to long terms there. Chips Kelly had gotten off with a light jail term and a fine.

It was too late in the season for wild flowers but cured bluestem, knee-high, grew on both sides of the trail. "Wait till you see it at our place, Donna," Tony boasted. "And wait till you see those yearlings Jim Pearson bought for us. It's a better deal than the one I tried to make with Frank Wagner." Jim Pearson was a top hand the real Jerry DeSpain had recommended. He'd been down at the Hollister ranch for five weeks, with a crew, stocking the place and putting up hay.

"All it needs now," Tony said, "is you and me."

Everything was right, this fall day on Paradise Prairie. When a flock of quail whirred up from the grass the team didn't even shy. Driving with one hand, Tony let the team walk. It was his world and Donna's, from now on. Tonight they'd stay at the Durwin place and tomorrow night at their own.

Center Point Large Print
600 Brooks Road / PO Box 1
Thorndike, ME 04986-0001 USA

(207) 568-3717

US & Canada:
1 800 929-9108
www.centerpointlargeprint.com